Dusty took Mikayla's mouth in an urgent kiss. He kissed her as if he was a starving man and she was a feast.

Mikayla responded with an enthusiasm he'd only dreamed about. She wrapped her arms around his neck and pulled him tight, parting her lips to accept his hot tongue as it explored every inch of her mouth.

Dusty picked up Mikayla and within seconds she was beneath him on the large four-poster bed. His blue-jean-clad legs pushed hers apart so that he could sink into her body. Dusty was awed by how well their bodies fit together. It was as if she were molded just for him. But there was only one potter that could create anything as divine as Mikayla Schroeder.

He let his tongue roll over her neck in featherlight touches, savoring the shift of her body as she pulsed with pleasure. He slid his hand between their bodies and almost groaned at the heat coming from her center. She wanted him as much as he wanted her.

Not sure he could wait much longer, Dusty sat back and pulled his polo shirt over his head, before scooping her up in his arms once more.

Mikayla followed Du[...]
She went to unsnap [...]
hands got there first [...]

"Let me," he whispe[...]

Books by Elaine Overton

Kimani Romance

Fever
Daring Devotion
His Holiday Bride
Seducing the Matchmaker
Sugar Rush
His Perfect Match
Miami Attraction

Kimani Arabesque

Promises of the Heart
Déjà Vu
Love's Inferno

ELAINE OVERTON

currently resides in the Detroit area with her son. She attended a local business college before entering the military and serving in the Gulf War.

She is an administrative assistant, currently working for an automotive-industry supplier and is an active member of Romance Writers of America.

MIAMI
Attraction

ELAINE OVERTON

KIMANI
PRESS

KIMANI PRESS™

Recycling programs
for this product may
not exist in your area.

ISBN-13: 978-0-373-86158-3

MIAMI ATTRACTION

Dear Reader,

Thank you for taking the time to read *Miami Attraction*. As we all know, everyone we meet comes from a different walk of life and a different background, and sometimes the parts of our pasts that we are most ashamed of are the parts that have made us stronger. They are the parts that have made us who we are today.

In Dusty and Mikayla's story I have tried to express exactly that sentiment. These two characters find a way to embrace their future together, but in order to do that they must first learn how to heal the pains of their past.

I hope you enjoy their story.

Take care,

Elaine

Chapter 1

Mikayla Shroeder stood outside the front door of her three-bedroom stucco bungalow in the South Beach neighborhood. She hesitated to put her key in the lock and open the door for fear of what awaited her on the other side.

She'd been gone from her home for a record seven days now, and despite the help she'd hired to deal with her *problem,* she held little hope much had changed in her absence. Still, she was near exhaustion and the thought of sleeping in her own bed tonight held too much appeal to resist. It was time to face the unavoidable.

On a deep sigh she placed the key in the lock, turned and steeled herself for what would come next. She pushed on the heavy oak door as it opened.

She waited. Nothing happened.

She pushed it even farther open until she could see

the entryway leading to the sunken living room. She entered the house, confused by the silence.

At first glance everything appeared to be *normal*. The small cherrywood table that decorated the foyer was once again lying on its side. The small glass vase that usually sat on the table was smashed, with bits of glass scattered across the light oak wood floor, interspersed with the wilted flowers that once occupied the vase.

"Hello?" Stepping over the glass, she closed the door behind her and moved farther into the house, walking toward the living room. The recently purchased orange pillows that were supposed to line the bright red, box-styled sofas were thrown about the room. The round glass coffee table was still centered between the sofas, but the stacks of her favorite travel books were falling over on themselves and spilling off the table.

Despite the disarray, which was expected, the stillness of the place bothered her the most.

"Kim?" Mikayla frowned to herself as her confusion grew and along with it, her concern. "Angel? Where's my sweet girl?"

Her calls were met with dead silence.

She walked along the short, cream, carpeted pathway that led around the sunken living room and rounded the corner into the kitchen.

The sink was full of dishes, except for the ones that had been pulled out of a bottom cabinet and tossed around the room. The dish towel was sprawled on the floor next to where both wood counter stools lay on their sides. The box of dog treats that usually sat in one corner of the counter was turned on its side and completely emptied.

Mikayla was crossing the room to pick up one of the stools when she heard the first sounds of life.

"Drop it!" A forceful, female voice came from the back of the bungalow. "I said drop it!"

Mikayla hurried toward the voice, passing through the elegant dining room and vaguely noticing the table and chairs were upright and properly positioned.

"Give it back! Bad!" The female voice was growing angrier. "Bad Angel!"

Mikayla rushed through the glass sliding doors that led to the backyard and pool patio, and stopped in her tracks.

"Bad Angel! Bad!" Kim Shapiro, her nineteen-year-old neighbor and dog sitter was standing, dripping wet beside the pool in a royal blue bikini bottom and nothing else. Her small hands were balled in fists at her side; her pretty face was twisted in an angry expression as she glared across the pool. "Drop it, Angel! I mean it!"

Mikayla followed the direction of Kim's death stare and knew what she'd find before her eyes landed on the large, scruffy, tan-colored dog standing on the other side of the pool. The dog's wet tail was wagging in excitement, her soaked fur dripping on the patio as a wet bikini top hung from her mouth.

"Oh, no," Mikayla groaned, knowing she'd just lost yet another dog sitter.

The small noise was enough to startle the teenager, and she covered her bare breasts with her arms. "Ms. Shroeder—I didn't hear you come in."

"It's okay. I can see you're busy." Mikayla started along the poolside toward Angel, who'd already dropped the bikini top and was charging in her direction.

Mikayla braced herself for the huge paws that landed on her shoulders a moment later, and positioned her feet to keep her balance. It had taken her months to learn that trick; Angel use to knock her down with little effort.

Kim seized the opportunity to rush around the pool and grab her top. "Aren't you back a little early?" She cast one last glare at Angel before turning her back to the pair and tying the halter top back on.

Mikayla looked at the dog's face now inches from her own, and found bright blue eyes blinking back at her and a pink tongue lolling to the side. Hot breath that smelled like day-old milk bones blew across her face.

Despite the scene she'd entered on, and Angel's penchant for trouble, Mikayla was satisfied that her pet had not been mistreated in her absence.

Rubbing the top of the shaggy head of her ill-behaved beast, she asked Kim, "How was everything this week?"

Kim turned with a false smile in place. "Great! Just great. Me and Angel had a great time. Didn't we, girl?"

"Down, Angel," Mikayla said, but Angel was too busy licking her face to hear her name being said. "Down, Angel!" Mikayla said again, with little reaction from the dog.

She took the large paws and forcefully removed them from her shoulders.

Not the slightest bit put off by the rebuke, Angel shuffled away to her favorite end of the pool and dived in.

"What happened?" Mikayla asked, taking in the

water-splattered patio, and various pool toys scattered around the area.

"We were in the pool—" Kim began to explain.

"She loves the pool," Mikayla interjected apologetically as she began to understand what had occurred.

"Yeah, I know." Kim gave the dog a long-suffering look. "Anyway, everything was fine and then I dived too hard, I guess, and my top slipped up—"

Mikayla stopped where she was bent over picking up a floaty. "Oh, dear." She muttered. "Angel grabbed it."

"It happened so fast!" Kim's blue eyes widened in renewed surprise. "Before I even realized what had happened she had it and was out of the pool." She sighed. "That's where you came in."

"I'm sorry about that. Angel feels that anything loose in the pool is, well…up for grabs." Mikayla bent and picked up a chew toy, but just then Angel came loping up, leaving a trail of water in her wake, and snatched the toy from Mikayla's hand. "I guess it's my fault. I've let her get away with it for so long."

"For the most part, she's a real sweetheart." Kim leaned forward and rubbed the dog's wet head. "Just…a little rambunctious."

"That's an understatement," Mikayla muttered. She glanced at the girl who, despite the bikini top incident, looked none the worse after a week with Angel, and decided now was as good a time as any to bring up her next trip. "Listen, Kim, I have another conference in a few weeks and—"

"I can't!" Kim blurted. "I have plans for that week."

I haven't even said which week.

A brief glimpse of what looked like embarrassment crossed the girl's face. "I mean, I'm going to be heading back to school soon. Spring break's almost over. I doubt if I'd be able to do it."

"I understand." Mikayla forced a smile. *Another one bites the dust.* She was running out of neighbors. Soon Angel's name and picture would be posted on the community board in front of the local library under the heading BEWARE. Then what was she supposed to do for dog sitters?

After all, Kim had been an unexpected prize. Mikayla and Angel had moved in a little over a year ago and with Kim being away at college most of the year, she'd somehow been spared the worst of the rumors about the new neighborhood nuisance, as Mikayla had heard her next-door neighbor refer to Angel.

When they'd run into Kim during one of their afternoon walks, Kim and Angel had taken to each other, and that was an excellent omen, considering how rare it was that Angel took to anyone.

Over the next few weeks, Mikayla had set out on a calculated campaign to win the girl over and it hadn't taken much since she already loved animals, and when Kim was around Angel was on her best behavior.

So, when she offered to pay Kim to stay at her house for a few days to take care of the dog, and Kim, like most college students, needed money, it had seemed like a match made in heaven.

But still, during the entire five-day trip, Mikayla could not get rid of the nagging feeling that she'd set Kim up to be a victim. During her motivation lectures to the gathering of aspiring writers, Mikayla's mind had wandered away on several occasions. And even during the book signing, she'd autographed a copy of her book "To Angel."

And when she'd arrived home today, she'd expected to find the same scene she'd found after returning from her last two trips. Turned-over tables and chairs, torn pillows and damp carpets. The fact the house still looked like a house was a testament to Kim's unique relationship with her pet. But that emphatic response had been enough to let her know they'd lost the last, best hope.

"Well, now that you're back, I'm gonna head home." Kim headed toward the glass doors leading into the house.

Mikayla looked down at her scruffy companion who was staring back at her with adoring eyes and a wagging tail, wanting to play.

"What am I gonna do with you?" Mikayla asked.

Angel's response was the accelerated wagging of the tail and a loud bark. Play was all she had on her mind.

At the glass doors, Kim paused. "Um…Ms. Shroeder?"

"Yes?"

"Have you ever thought of sending Angel to an obedience school?"

"It's crossed my mind," Mikayla said, finding no need to mention that she'd tried it with three different schools, all of which had returned both her money and her dog and declared the task impossible. But Kim didn't need to know all that. She was already enough of a lost cause as it was.

"Just thought I'd ask. I'll just go grab my bag out

of the guest room," Kim said and headed toward the bedrooms. Angel glanced at the girl and then back at Mikayla, torn as to which to follow.

Mikayla watched the dog make her decision as she plopped down on her wide bottom. "What am I going to do with you, huh?"

Angel looked up at her owner with big, innocent eyes. A few minutes later Mikayla was in the kitchen, standing with the fridge door open, looking for something to eat when Kim entered, carrying the overnight tote she'd collected from the guest room.

"Here you go." Mikayla turned and handed the girl an envelope. "I gave you a little more than we agreed on." She nodded down at Angel who was sitting on her foot. "I know she can be a handful."

"You didn't have to do that—but thank you."

Kim accepted the envelope and looked down at the dog with gentle eyes. "She's certainly high-strung, but she is a sweetheart. Just mischievous."

The young woman's compassionate response made Mikayla regret losing her even more.

"See you later, Ms. Shroeder." Kim paused again. "You know, I've heard about this dog trainer in Davies. Dr. Dusty Warren. He's supposed to be some kind of dog whisperer, you know—gifted with animals."

Despite her failure with trainers, Mikayla's interest was sparked nonetheless. "Really?"

"Yeah, my aunt had an aggressive mastiff and from what she said this guy worked wonders."

"Dusty Warren, you said?" Mikayla dug out some leftover sandwich meats, cheese slices and mayonnaise from the fridge.

"Yeah, he's a really renowned vet, and from what my aunt said he has this huge sprawling ranch down in Davies with a full-size hospital and everything. I mean, if you ever consider getting her some training that would be a place to start. Anyway, just thought I'd mention it." The girl headed to the door, holding up the envelope. "Thanks for the money."

"Thank you for taking care of Angel!" Mikayla called out.

Angel barely acknowledged the girl's departure. Her full attention was centered on the sandwich being stacked on the marble island counter top. Her fluffy tail wagged as Mikayla began to cut it in half.

"Dr. Dusty Warren, huh?" she muttered to herself. "A dog whisperer." Hearing a slight whimper, she looked to see Angel wagging her tail and glancing back between the sandwich and Mikayla.

Mikayla raised an eyebrow. "And exactly why do you think you deserve this after your behavior this morning?"

Angel glanced at her expectantly and returned her attention to the sandwich.

"I wonder if this Dr. Warren is really any different from the others."

As if sensing her chances of getting some of the sandwich were slimming, Angel made another whimpering sound.

"Oh, all right." Mikayla dropped half the sandwich into Angel's food bowl. "Although you really don't deserve it."

Angel rushed to the bowl and began gobbling down the sandwich.

Picking up the remaining half of the sandwich, Mikayla collected her computer carry case from where she'd left it near the front door and headed to her study. Before she got her hopes up again, she wanted to do a little research on this Dr. Dusty Warren.

Chapter 2

Dr. Dusty Warren had just finished the procedure of neutering a one-year-old Yorkie, and was in the process of tying off his final stitch in his operating room when he heard the commotion coming from the outer offices of his veterinarian hospital.

He frowned at his nurse, but Nurse Francine Weathers shrugged in confusion. Dusty forced himself to ignore the unidentified noises and focus on his patient.

Then a loud crash, followed by a screech, a scream and an irate voice caused him to put down the instrument and go to the door.

He opened it just as a bolt of reddish-gold fur shot past the door with a long, red cloth trailing behind. He recognized the blur as a dog right before two of his staff came charging around the corner, chasing the dog.

"Come back here, you hell hound!" His front-desk receptionist, Hannah, called, sounding more angry than he'd ever heard her before. Hannah was the most cheerful employee he had.

Right behind Hannah was Tim, one of his property caretakers, and Tim's reaction was different than that of Hannah's. Tim was laughing so hard he was out of breath and bracing himself against the wall to keep from falling.

"What the hell is going on?" Dusty asked Tim.

Tim's eyes widened, noticing his boss standing in the doorway of the operating room.

"Sorry, Dr. Warren, a dog got loose."

"A dog?"

"A new patient. Hannah was just checking her in when—"

A blue-jeans-clad woman came charging around the same corner as the others and did not even hesitate as she rushed past both Dusty and Tim, following in the wake of Hannah and the dog.

A slight breeze of perfume floated on the air as she passed, but the woman was moving so fast Dusty barely saw her face. The snug fit of the jeans around her curvy hips would've been noticeable even in the dark.

"Who was that?" he asked Tim, who still hadn't moved from his position on the opposite wall.

"That's the dog's owner." Tim looked down the hall where the three had disappeared around the corner. "It's Mikayla Shroeder."

"The author?"

"In the flesh." Tim nodded.

Dusty shook his head, trying to shake off his growing confusion. "Can you finish up here?" he called to Nurse Fran over his shoulder.

"No problem," she called back.

Dusty let go of the swinging door, removed his latex gloves and went after the two women and the dog, motioning for Tim to follow.

Dusty thought about the large size of the animal that had rushed by earlier. "Is the dog dangerous?" he asked, taking long strides.

"No," Tim answered a few steps behind him, "just ill-mannered. That thing she has in his mouth is Hannah's new dress. She bought it for a party she's going to tonight with her *new boyfriend.*"

Dusty glanced over his shoulder at his young care-taker, remembering that only recently he and Hannah had stopped dating.

"She had just taken it out of the bag to show some of us and then the phone rang." Tim continued. "She laid it on the desk, and out of nowhere the dog grabbed it and took off."

Dusty came around the corner. He stopped dead in his tracks, leaving Tim to put on his brakes to avoid running into the back of him. They were in the pen area and the other dogs locked in the cages were going crazy with the sudden infusion of activity around them.

Before Dusty were his receptionist, Hannah, and the dog's owner, both flanking the dog. To be fair, the scruffy, mangy mutt barely qualified as a canine. The large dog had dirty, gold-colored, matted fur. She had the large, muscular build and square-shaped head of a Saint Bernard, but the pointed features and blue eyes of a husky. Independently, both were beautiful species of dogs, but combined in this two-hundred-pound monstrosity it seemed an abomination.

Watching the two women, its whole body vibrated with excitement. The dog stood in a wide-legged stance with a tattered red cloth clamped between its teeth, shining blue eyes looking for any small opportunity to escape.

In the cacophony of barks and howls, Dusty heard what sounded like a muffled cry and realized it was coming from his receptionist.

"Oh, what's the use, it's ruined!" Hannah's shoulders slumped, her guard dropped, and the dog seized the opportunity, ducking between her legs only to be grabbed by the collar and tackled by Tim.

"I'm so sorry." The other woman put her arms around Hannah's shoulders, and Dusty found his eyes once again drawn to her fitted jeans. "I'll replace it—today. Just tell me where you bought it and the size and I'll pick up another today."

"You can't!" Hannah cried harder. "It was the last one, I found it on the clearance rack."

Dusty glanced back to where the dog was wiggling and squirming to get free from Tim's tight hold around its body. The animal's legs were spread wide as it kicked and pawed in every direction. Tim hauled the animal over to an empty carry case and pushed her into it headfirst and latched the box closed.

Angel began to revolt, barking and scratching at the sides of the box. Hearing her pet's cry for help, Mikayla left the young woman's side and kneeled beside the box.

She attempted to comfort Angel with shushing noises. Seeing it was not working, she sighed. "Sorry, baby, but you brought this on yourself."

Meanwhile, Tim had circled back around and replaced Mikayla, wrapping his arm around Hannah's shoulder in an attempt to console her over the loss of her new dress.

Between the howling animals and the crying receptionist, Dusty had had enough. He walked over to the woman kneeling beside the cage and offered his hand to bring her to her feet. Mikayla accepted the helping hand, and as she stood she came eye-to-eye with the doctor.

Dusty forgot his train of thought. His staff, the barking dogs, everything fell away. All he could focus on were eyes the color of September's fall leaves just as they began to turn that rich, deep brown. There was aged knowledge in those eyes that did not go with the beautiful, youthful face in which they were contained. She was what the elders called an *old soul*. A person wise beyond their years, and he was curious to know what had given such a beautiful young woman such sad eyes.

Feeling her tug, he realized he was still holding her hand and quickly released it.

He cleared his throat and put on his professional voice. "Hello, I'm Dr. Dusty Warren." He introduced himself to the woman.

"Mikayla Shroeder." She smiled. "Sorry to cause your staff so much trouble, but I guess you can see why we're here." She gestured to the dog. "This is Angel, and as you can see she is in desperate need of some training, and I was told you're the best."

Dusty smiled. "You've certainly come to the right place. Tim, please put the dog in room three."

But Tim and Hannah had their heads bent together, talking in whispers. Rather than call him again, Dusty pushed the wheeled case himself. "This way." He gestured for Mikayla to go ahead of him.

"I apologize again. I don't know what got into her." Mikayla was speaking over her shoulder as she moved back into the main hospital.

"Well, let's go find out, shall we?" Dusty struggled to keep his head up and avoid looking at those form-fitting jeans and how they moved with her body.

"I think you may have accidentally done Tim a good service," Dusty said, closing the door behind him. "That dress was for Hannah's date with a *new* guy."

"Aaahhh," Mikayla said. "With Tim being the *old* guy, I presume?"

"Exactly."

Dusty parked the case by the table, and Angel was sitting quietly inside, having accepted her temporary fate. Dusty reached over to the wall and took down a leash.

He opened the cage and hooked the leash to her collar before Angel even realized what he was doing. But once the collar was attached she began bouncing around inside. Even with her standing a few feet away, Dusty could feel the tension in Mikayla.

Once the dog was out of the cage and climbing all over Dusty, Mikayla released a breath she'd been holding.

"She likes you." The slight surprise in Mikayla's voice indicated that this was not typically the case.

Dusty pushed Angel back down on her bottom and began trying to examine her, while she continued to climb on him, attempting to put her paws over his shoulders. All of a sudden her busy motion stopped and she sat down on her rump, tail wagging, but beyond that she was calm.

Dusty looked at the dog and was surprised to see her just watching him in silence. "She seems in good health."

After much resistance, he managed to get her mouth open and looked at her teeth. "What is she, about six? Six and a half?"

"I think so."

He glanced at Mikayla and looked away. *What a beauty,* he thought, trying to keep his mind on the dog.

He knew about the author and motivational speaker, Mikayla Shroeder. Who didn't? In fact, he'd read her first book a few years ago. He'd picked it up at the airport, just wanting something to read on the plane while traveling to a veterinarian conference in Portland, Oregon, not realizing at the time that it was Christian inspirational nonfiction.

The book, *Reclaiming Your Soul,* had been a national bestseller within weeks of coming out, and launched the formerly unknown author into instant superstardom. That day in the airport, he had wanted to see what all the fuss was about. In fact, as far as he knew the book was still selling in record volumes.

Surprisingly, he'd enjoyed reading it at the time, but he had given little thought to the author, and what thought he'd given had not come anywhere close to the gorgeous, young woman standing in his office.

She'd only written the one book that he knew of, but

nowadays you couldn't turn on the radio without hearing a promotion for one of her upcoming seminars.

He'd assumed she was older. Much older. Why, he wasn't sure, just something about the way she wrote spoke of a maturity beyond her years. He thought about the book he'd read and didn't think there'd been an author photo along with the brief bio.

He was so occupied by his thoughts of Mikayla that what came next took him by surprise. Angel sprang at him in joyful delight, all two hundred pounds of her, and together they hit the floor with Dusty on the bottom.

Before he knew what had happened, Angel was standing on his chest, smiling down at him. She barked once, a loud, happy bark as if to declare she'd won.

"Angel!" Mikayla was pulling on the leash, trying to get the dog off him, but Dusty was more successful in just pushing her to the side and climbing to his feet. Except for a bruised ego, he was none the worse off.

"Bad girl!" Mikayla was scolding her, even as she petted her head. Dusty wondered if she understood how contradictory her actions were.

He dusted himself off. "You shouldn't do that."

"Do what?"

"You're disciplining her with words, but rewarding her with action." He motioned to where her hand was running over the dog's head. Angel's tail wagged as she enjoyed the petting.

Mikayla looked down at her hand as if it had taken on a life of it's own. "I hadn't even realized it." She snatched back her hand. "It's just habit."

Dusty glanced down at the dog who was once again

sitting, this time at her master's side, her tail still wagging happily.

Dusty thought he better lay down the ground rules now. He'd seen this before. People who could not bear the idea of being apart from their pets for any amount of time. Just watching her behavior with the dog, Dusty thought Mikayla Shroeder might be one of those people.

"Ms. Shroeder—"

"Mikayla."

"Mikayla, you need to understand that my training methods are different from others. If I accept Angel as a client, she has to stay here with me."

Her eyes widened. "For how long?"

"Eight weeks."

"Eight weeks? Why so long?"

He braced his weight against the examination table and folded his arms across his chest. "What I do is less training and more deprogramming. I need to be her complete focus for a while. After two weeks, you can come visit her and then after that I need you to come in once a week for training."

"What kind of training?" she asked.

"You have to understand that Angel is half the problem. You're the other half. Your behavior toward her has to change as much as her behavior toward you."

She glanced down at her dog, who gazed up at her with adoring eyes. "I don't know about this. Eight weeks is a long time. We haven't been separated that long, since…I just don't know."

Dusty caught the pause, but said nothing. Most people who came to him never went through with the program for this very reason. They did not want to be separated from their pet for such an extended amount of time. But separating them was the only way to get the dog's complete attention, and getting the dog's complete attention was the way to retrain them.

"I tell you what." He walked over to her and took Angel's leash. "How about I give you a tour of the hospital and training facility and then you make up your mind?"

Chapter 3

Dusty led her down a series of hallways, pointing out the various rooms to her, showing her the hospital was a lot bigger than it looked from the entrance.

"We are a full-service hospital and can accommodate up to twenty-five patients overnight."

"Are you the only doctor?"

"Yes. I do allow other local vets to use the facility on occasion. We have two operating rooms, both are state-of-the-art in their components."

The pride in his voice was evident as he guided her around his hospital, and Mikayla couldn't help but be impressed by the place and the man.

They reached the back entrance where a set of automated double doors led to the emergency entrance. As they walked out of the back entrance it was like they were walking into another world.

From the front entrance the Warren ranch looked

like a comfortable tract of land, big enough to hold the hospital and make a kennel, but behind the hospital its secret was revealed. The place was huge.

She stood on a slight incline overlooking acre after acre of green, open fields. In the distance, she could see another tall two-level building, made of the same light brick that the hospital was made of. Beside the two-story building was a smaller building that Mikayla could not quite make out from the distance.

He gestured to two golf carts sitting nearby. "If you want we can take one of the carts, but if you don't mind I would rather walk." He gestured to Angel, whom he still held by the leash. "Give her a chance to burn off some of that energy."

As if sensing the possibility, Angel was pulling at the leash, straining to get out in the open field.

"Lead the way," Mikayla said, and they headed across the field.

The more she saw, the more impressed Mikayla became. On one edge sat a stable and barn. Several horses pranced and stood in the gigantic pen just outside it. On the opposite end sat a large, three-story brick house.

Once they started walking, Angel stopped pulling at the leash and skipped along, sniffing at various things in the grass and taking in her surroundings. It didn't escape Mikayla's notice that Dusty seemed to have her pet well in hand.

Maybe, she thought, his way of doing things, keeping Angel on the ranch for eight weeks, would work. At least, no one had ever tried anything like that before. And she seemed satisfied to stay at his side.

"Do you board horses here?" she asked, gesturing to the stables.

"Yes, but we also raise them. I have some of the finest trainers in the country and three young colts, one of which I think could take a title."

"Vet, dog trainer and horse breeder. Wow," she said with a shake of her head. "You're a busy man."

"And you're a busy lady. I have to confess I've read your book."

"Oh? What did you think?"

"It was excellent, very thought provoking. It's just you seem too young to have such an in-depth understanding of human nature."

A brief sadness crossed her eyes, and Dusty regretted his words.

"Hard times do not have an age limit." She pointed toward the large house. "Is that your home?"

He nodded, his attention distracted by Angel who'd gotten wrapped up in the leash. "Yes. I have three dogs of my own, by the way. So along with the dogs in the kennel, Angel will have lots of company and opportunity to interact with other dogs."

"That would be good. She doesn't get that chance very often."

Before she realized it, they had reached the training facility. She glanced back up the hill where the hospital sat, still amazed that the large building somehow hid all this from the main road.

Dusty introduced her to the staff of trainers and gave her an overview of what a typical day would be like for Angel. He showed her the area she would be kept in, and Mikayla had to admit that as far as kennels went, this was quite elegant, with padded floors and more toys than Angel could ever play with.

Outside, she was shown the large play area where several dogs lounged, enjoying the sun.

"Most of the dogs spend the majority of their time outside, so don't think she will be sitting in a kennel all day."

She shook her head. "No, I didn't think that. You have a great place here and I'm sure she would be fine. It's just we've never been apart for very long periods of time."

Dusty stopped walking and turned to face her. "Mikayla, I can help Angel, but you're going to have to trust me. I know eight weeks seems like a long time, but it's the minimal amount of time necessary to deprogram her bad behavior."

Mikayla glanced around once more, and could find no fault with the ranch. She looked at Dusty and could find no fault with the man. "Okay." She nodded.

She bent to Angel's level, and the dog pulled on the leash to get to her. "I wish you could understand that I am not abandoning you." She kissed the dog's furry head and fought back the tears.

"I'll take good care of her. You can come see her in two weeks."

She stood. "I know."

"Let me take her inside to Sam and I'll be right back."

She nodded and looked away as Dusty led Angel back inside. At the door the dog stopped and looked back at her, expecting Mikayla to follow, and when she did not,

Angel turned to go back to her, prompting Dusty to tug on her leash.

The dog finally surrendered and followed the man inside. Once they were out of sight, Mikayla walked to the six-foot fence surrounding the play area and released the tears she'd been holding back.

She knew her behavior would seem extreme to Dr. Warren or anyone there. After all, they would only be separated for eight weeks. But no one else understood what this separation meant. It wasn't just a few weeks apart, it was a broken promise.

Only one other soul in the world knew the truth, that the relationship between her and Angel went deeper than just owner and pet. They were best friends. Not only friends, they were each others saviors.

On the worst night of her life, five years ago, as she lay bleeding to death in a deserted alley, she'd made a promise to the stray dog that rescued her from her attacker. The dog, even after the attack was over, stood over her wounded body like a sentinel, watching, guarding from all comers.

The dog refused to leave her side, even as the blood from her own injuries coated her fur and dripped onto the concrete. That night, she'd promised the dog a home for life. No one would ever separate them. And now, for the first time she was about to break that promise.

Sure, she took trips to do speaking engagements, but Angel had always remained safe and sound in her own home, knowing Mikayla would return. But this was different. This time, Angel would be living away from her home for two months, and Mikayla had no way to assure her she would return.

She felt like the worst kind of betrayer. Hearing the door open behind her, she swiped at her eyes. This was going to be the longest two weeks of her life.

"Okay, she's all settled in." Dusty came up beside her, and the surprised look on his face told her she had not gotten rid of all the evidence of her sorrow.

"Hey, relax. I promise you, Angel's going to be just fine. I've been training dogs for over ten years. I know what I'm doing."

She forced a smile. "I'm sure you do."

"Come on." He gestured to a nearby golf cart. "I want to show you something."

The pair climbed in and Dusty guided the cart toward his house. The closer they came to the house, the more her tension grew.

"Where are we going?" she asked, looking directly at his house in the distance.

Despite the fact that he was certain she knew, still he pointed to the house. "My home. I have some friends there I want you to meet."

Her eyes widened in terror, and Dusty could literally feel her fear like it was a tangible thing.

"What's wrong?"

"What do you mean friends you want me to meet—I just met you!"

"It's okay, trust me." Dusty was split between her reaction and the strong emotions swirling in the atmosphere around his head. It was the most bizarre thing, but he knew with complete certainty he was *feeling* her emotions. And what she was *feeling* was not good.

"Trust you? I don't even know you!"

He stopped the cart, and she was instantly out of it, walking quickly back up the hill toward the hospital.

"Mikayla!" he called to her, then turned the cart around and followed until he could come up beside her. "Did I say something wrong?"

She shook her head. "I just remembered something I have to do."

He stopped the cart again. "I just wanted to introduce you to my dogs!" he called after her.

She stopped in her tracks. She turned to look at him. "Your dogs?"

He hopped out of the cart and walked to her. "I thought if you saw them and heard how far they had come it would be encouraging to you."

The heavy air surrounding them began to thin as she smiled. "Your *dogs*."

The calm expression on her pretty face could not wipe away the terror she'd felt a moment ago. He'd felt it as surely as she did. It was the strangest phenomenon he'd ever experienced, but he knew it was real.

He gestured to the cart. "Do you have time?"

She nodded and climbed back into the cart.

As they approached the house, Mikayla could see it was even bigger than she'd thought. "Wow, what a beautiful home."

"Thank you." He stepped out of the cart and waited for her to join him. Together they went along the side of the large house, to the backyard where three dogs, a Labrador retriever, a German shepherd and a Chihuahua all lay on the large open deck, bathing in the sun.

The three together, so different and yet seeming in

perfect synch, made a comical trio, and Mikayla couldn't help but smile.

Dusty gestured to the open area around his house. "As you can see, there is no fence to keep them in. In fact, they are pretty much given free run of the ranch, but nonetheless most days this is where you will find them.

"The big guy is Athos." He gestured to the German shepherd. "The Labrador is Porthos, and—"

"And let me guess, the Chihuahua is Aramis."

He smiled in return. "Good guess."

"The Three Musketeers."

"After watching them together for a while, I could come up with no better names."

"Did you get them all at the same time?"

"Yes, and…" His smile faded. "And all were meant to be bait in dog fights."

She glanced back at the dogs resting on the porch. Only Aramis seemed to be aware of their presence. He lifted his little head and sniffed the air. Satisfied with what he found, he plopped is head back down on the deck.

"When they were rescued, they were all slated to be put down for different reasons. Aramis there was deemed in too bad a shape to survive. Athos had become extremely aggressive and Porthos is said to have psychological problems.

"Even though they thought I was crazy I talked the rescue shelter into letting me adopt them. I brought them home and worked with them. With a little love, time and attention I made them into the worthless fleabags you see before you."

She laughed. "Wow, what an improvement."

His smiled faded. "Actually, it is."

He crossed the yard and once he came into their line of vision all three dogs rose to greet him. "My point is that with a little love, time and attention I think any dog can be retrained." He sat down on a stair and the dogs surrounded him, with Aramis wiggling past the two bigger dogs to climb onto Dusty's lap. "You just have to give them a sense of security and safety. Something these dogs had never had."

Mikayla followed him to the porch and the three dogs wandered over to sniff out the stranger. "I'm sorry, I hope I didn't give you the impression that I doubted your level of compassion. I don't. It's just..." She paused, petting Porthos's soft gold head and thinking of how much to say to this man who was still a stranger. "Just like you chose their names because it suited them. I named her Angel for a reason."

Dusty watched her as some light of recognition came into his eyes. "I understand." He nodded. "Just give me two weeks and see if you don't see a world of difference."

She frowned and rubbed Athos under his furry chin.

"What?" Dusty was watching her with narrowed eyes. "What are you thinking?"

She shrugged. "It's just—I know Angel, and she has a tendency to be...how do I put it? Stubborn."

Dusty smiled. "So am I."

"And don't let her scruffy appearance fool you—she's very intelligent."

"Most dogs are."

"And—" Mikayla found herself wanting to warn Dusty but was unsure of the words "—she can be a bit sneaky."

He smirked. "Again, most dogs are." He leaned forward. "Look, Mikayla, I haven't met a dog I couldn't train, and I'm sure Angel will be no exception."

Mikayla thought about her resourceful dog and all the clever little stunts she'd pulled over the years on dog sitters and dog trainers alike. She already knew it was going to be a long two weeks. Still, she decided, this man seemed different, and therefore deserved the benefit of the doubt.

She forced a smile. "I'm sure you're right."

Chapter 4

"Dusty Warren?" Kandi Martin, Mikayla's literary agent and manager, took another bite of her Caesar salad, a slight frown creasing her brow. "I've heard that name before, but I can't remember where."

"Well, he's well respected in his field and Angel's last, best hope." Mikayla took another sip of the cheese soup she'd chosen as an appetizer. "You should see his facility. It's really state-of-the-art. I've never seen anything like it."

Kandi glanced across the table at her friend. "Sounds like an interesting man. Is he married?"

Mikayla returned the glance, knowing what her friend was asking. "Don't even go there. This is just about Angel." She shrugged. "Besides, when would I have time for a man?"

"Some things you *make* time for." Reaching into the basket on the center of the table, Kandi took a roll and tore it in half. "It's about balance." She held up the two parts of the roll. "The ying and the yang. Work versus play. If you ask me, you have way too much of one and not enough of the other."

Mikayla reached across the table and snatched one of the halves. "Well, I didn't ask you, did I?" To emphasize her point, she bit off the roll before placing it on her soup saucer.

As the waiter arrived with their entrées, and removed the soup and salad dishes, Kandi dug around in her large tote bag. "By the way, I received this the other day." She handed Mikayla an elegant cream envelope.

"What's this?" Mikayla opened the envelope and read the enclosed card. It was an invitation to speak at an AKA dinner at Bethune-Cookman University. "Oh, definitely." She handed the invitation back.

"That's another one of your problems, you spend too much of your time in all-female groupings. How are you gonna meet a potential lover like that?"

"First of all, let me restate, I *am not* looking for a lover. Second, it's not my fault mostly women show up for my lectures."

"Riiiggghhhttt," Kandi muttered, cutting into her chicken parmesan.

"What's that supposed to mean?"

Kandi looked up at her friend with a tilted head and a knowing expression. "Come on, this is me you're talking to. Don't try to tell me you don't enjoy getting up in front of a group of women and giving your little I-am-woman-hear-me-roar pep talk. You love it."

"If by that you mean, do I enjoy empowering women who have been victimized in their own lives for far too long, then yes, I do." She leaned forward, feeling defensive about her work. "And if my book can help even one woman regain control of her life, then—"

"Hang on, Sojourner." Kandi held up her hands as if to ward off an attack. "Don't get me wrong, I love what you do." She reached across the table and took Mikayla's hand. "And more importantly, I understand *why* you do it. I'm just saying you need more in your life than just this...this one-woman crusade you're on."

Mikayla sat back in her chair. "I do have more in my life than that."

Kandi's mouth twisted in a smirk. "Correction, more than a crusade—and a mangy mutt for companionship."

Mikayla frowned. "She's not mangy, she just has weird fur." She shook her head in confusion, her mind running off in a new direction. "I swear I've tried every dog shampoo known to man, and nothing will make her hair lie down like a regular dog."

Kandi shook the hand she was still holding to regain her friend's attention. "Hello? Enough about Angel's bad hair—I'm talking about you."

"Kandi, I appreciate all your help and advice, but believe me when I say I like my life just the way it is."

Kandi let go of her friend's hand and turned her attention to slicing up her chicken parmesan. "That's because you don't know any better. You've never had a normal relationship with a man, so you can't possibly know what you're missing."

The sudden silence caught her attention and she looked up to find Mikayla looking at her with a betrayed expression.

Her first instinct was to apologize for hurting her friend, but then she paused. As a policy, Kandi made a point of never apologizing for the truth, and if anyone needed to hear the truth it was Mikayla.

What started as a working relationship five years ago when Kandi signed Mikayla to a book contract had blossomed into one of the dearest relationships in her life, and she loved the younger woman sitting across from her like a little sister. But her little sister had scars. Scars left over from a vicious attack and the life before it. And until Mikayla confronted the ghost of her past those scars would never heal.

After the silence lingered a bit, Kandi muttered, "You know I don't apologize for the truth."

"*Your truth* is subjective," Mikayla countered.

"What's that supposed to mean?"

"As long as I was pumping out bestsellers you couldn't care less about my loveless lifestyle. Now that I've hit a wall, what's your sage advice? Get a lover."

Kandi pointed her fork at Mikayla. "That is so unfair. This is not the first time we've had this conversation. And it's not like I brought this up."

"Well, I certainly didn't!"

Kandi placed her fork on the table and folded her hands under her chin. "Describe this veterinarian."

"What?"

"The vet, Angel's best and last blah, blah, blah. Describe him. What does he look like?"

"How did we get back to him?"

Kandi arched an eyebrow. "That's where this conversation started, and that's where it will end. Now, describe him."

Mikayla shrugged. "I don't know. Good-looking, I guess."

"Be specific." Kandi picked up a forkful of steam cooked string beans. "You're a writer for goodness' sake, give me some details."

Mikayla sighed. "Fine. Let me think." She cut up her salmon and pulled to the forefront of her mind the face she'd been trying not to remember for the past week.

"Okay, he's got a caramel-brown complexion—no, wait. More like molasses when you heat it up, and it has deep, rich, brown coloring you can almost taste even before the sweet smell reaches your nose. And speaking of smell, my Lord, that man smells good." She frowned. "Which is amazing considering the fact he works with animals all day. But get within a few feet of him and his cologne. Just, mmmm…"

Mikayla closed her eyes and took a deep breath. "I've got to find out the name of his cologne." She chuckled. "Maybe I'll buy a bottle for myself and just keep it on my dresser. It really *is* a wonderful smell. Probably won't smell as good in the bottle as it does on him, though." She opened her eyes to find Kandi watching her with a bemused expression. "What?"

"Nothing. Go on, caramel-brown and smells good. What about his eyes?"

"Deep brown, chocolate-brown, like dark pools, but not so dark you can't see his bright pupils, and there is something else, as well. Just around the edges of his pupils are these unexpected flecks of gold. You know, they say you can see a person's soul through their eyes. If that's true, he has a compassionate soul."

She frowned again. "But I guess he would have to, considering—again—he works with animals all day."

"Nose?" Kandi asked, her attention focused on her meal.

"Straight, strong, average, neat." Mikayla smiled. "With the slightest little upturn on the tip. Adorable, really."

"Mouth?"

"Perfect heart shape. Beautiful. Full, but not overly so, just enough to make them kissable." She sighed again. "You should see his smile. It's amazing. It's like his whole face is transformed from just good-looking to stunning when he smiles. It makes you want to smile and you don't even know why." She laughed. "And on top of all that, he has the nerve to have dark red hair."

"Red?"

"Yeah, more like a dark, dusty, blondish-red. But he wears it close cut. You probably wouldn't notice except his eyebrows are the same color and when you meet him your attention is immediately drawn to those compassionate eyes."

"I wonder if that's where he got his name?"

"You know, I hadn't thought about it." Mikayla shrugged. "Maybe."

The two women ate in silence for several minutes before Mikayla said, "Okay, so maybe I do find him attractive, but so what? That doesn't change anything. All I want from this man is a manageable pet. I'm not interested in complicating my life with a relationship right now. I've got too much other stuff going on."

Kandi continued to eat, saying nothing.

"And besides, he probably already has a woman. Hell,

he may even be married and just doesn't wear a ring." She huffed. "Yeah, sounds about right, considering my taste in men." She stabbed at her salmon. "And who's to say he would even be interested? He probably flirts with every woman that comes into his clinic as a matter of habit."

Kandi continued to eat, seeming oblivious to her friend's conflicts.

"Using that damn smile of his like a weapon," Mikayla muttered, making minced meat of her salmon. "Probably thinks he can have any woman he wants."

After several more minutes had passed as the two ate in silence, Mikayla looked up and asked, "What were we talking about before?"

Kandi smiled. "I think we were deciding who brought up the topic of you needing a lover."

Mikayla's eyes narrowed menacingly on her friend's face. "You know, sometimes I can't stand you."

"I know." Kandi continued to smile. "I love you, too."

Chapter 5

Over the next two weeks, try as she might, Mikayla could not seem to shake off her most recent conversation with Kandi. She found Dusty Warren intruding on her thoughts more and more. It had been a long time since she'd been so attracted to a man, but there was just something about him. Those compassionate eyes, his smile, even the gentle way he handled Angel after she'd caused such chaos in his clinic. And the way he looked at her, there was no denying his interest. But was she ready for that?

So much had changed over the past five years and yet so much had stayed the same. For instance, during those two weeks Angel was with Dusty, Mikayla hardly slept. The days were lonely but bearable, but at night the same creaking, cracking noises that she heard every night since she'd moved into the house a year ago suddenly took on ominous tones. Every time a car would drive down the street and the light would shine into her bedroom window she would awaken with a start.

She'd known living without Angel would be hard company wise. After all, Angel had been her constant companion for the past five years, but she had not anticipated the return of the *fear*.

The same fear she'd experienced when she first arrived in Miami from Atlantic City and settled into their first home. Although she never told Kandi, a small part of Mikayla had always believed the man who attacked her, Vega, would hunt her down and finish the job after his trial ended in a hung jury. Her only comfort had been the knowledge that he would have to go through Angel to do it. After their first encounter, Mikayla was certain Vega would not want to tango with Angel again.

But without the sound of Angel's claws clacking against the vinyl floor in the kitchen as she patrolled from room to room every night, that comfort no longer existed. The *fear* had returned.

She lay wake at night listening to the sounds of the dark, and praying she was alone. And after just two weeks, she wasn't sure she could live like that for six more days, let alone six more weeks. Whether Dusty had been successful in retraining her or not, Mikayla was strongly considering bringing her pet home.

Which was why Mikayla doubted she was ready to return Dusty's obvious interest, or any other man's for that matter. Just look at the way she'd reacted when he took her to meet his dogs. As soon as he turned that cart in the direction of his house the fear had crept into her being. She'd managed to conquer it, as she had to so often. But still, to her embarrassment, he'd gotten a brief glimpse of her terror.

How was she to have any kind of a relationship with a man when every time he touched her she froze up?

No, despite whatever attraction she had for the good doctor, what she told Kandi was right. The only thing she wanted from Dusty Warren was a well-managed pet.

On her first visitation day Mikayla awoke with the excitement of a child on Christmas morning. Not only was she going to get to see Angel today, but before that she had a seminar in Fort Lauderdale she was really looking forward to.

She dressed in a dark suit and put her hair up in a French roll. She tried to cover the bags under her eyes with makeup but there was only so much Cover Girl bronzer could do.

As she applied the makeup in the bathroom mirror, she stopped for a moment and just examined her reflection. She'd come so far from the girl she once was. Her face was thinner, her hair shorter, and much lighter than before...how different she looked now. She wondered if her friends back in her old neighborhood in New Jersey would even recognize her?

She thought about those friends and wondered where they were today. The group of girls she'd hung out with, they'd all had so little, and hungered for so much. It was hard being poor in a place like Atlantic City. Watching the high rollers come and go in their expensive cars and expensive clothes, and there they were, just some poor locals craving a taste of that life.

Mikayla briefly wondered about her mother; it was not with the love of a child for a parent, but more idle curiosity. It had been a long time since Mikayla had loved her mother. Back before Mikayla came into puberty and the full extent of her future beauty began to shine through.

Instead of taking pride in her beautiful child, Regina Wilson had seen her daughter as a future rival for the male attention she enjoyed, and treated her only child as such. Even going so far as attempting to sell fifteen-year-old Mikayla to what she thought was a pimp and who turned out to be an undercover cop.

Mikayla knew nothing of her mother's plan until the cops came to take her into protective services. Three ounces of cocaine. That's what her mother valued her life at.

Mikayla was turned over to a foster care family that was already overloaded with the eight other foster children living in the home. But this arrangement worked out well for Mikayla because it allowed her to come and go as she pleased.

Even the memories felt like she was looking at someone else's life. She applied a thin coat of lipstick, straightened up the house a little, and taking her attaché, headed out to the car. She was due in Fort Lauderdale in less than an hour.

When her friend, Nisha, told her how much she could make stripping at the Godiva club where she worked, Mikayla had not believed it. But when Nisha later that year bought a sixty-thousand-dollar car at age eighteen, Mikayla was convinced.

She took the stage name Tangie after the nickname a

former boyfriend had given her. He'd claimed she was just the right combination of sugar and salt. Before long Tangie found it was not just the money she enjoyed, but the addictive feeling of power her beauty gave her over men. It didn't take her long to realize that with a smile and the promise of more, there was little she could not have.

Nisha had also given her a piece of advice that Mikayla had brushed off and would later regret not heeding. *Make sure they know you're teasing.*

Nisha had warned that as long as the patrons understood it was just a game of cat and mouse everybody went home happy. But when the men that came to the club began to believe the dancers liked them, things could get complicated. When one of the club's regulars brought her a pair of four-carat diamond earrings, Mikayla had let that bit of advice go in one ear and out the other.

His name was Vega, or at least that's what he told the girls to call him, and when he started coming to the club it was once or twice a week until it was almost every night.

He would sit at the bar and watch Tangie with an obsessive intensity. An intensity so fierce the bouncer, T.J., had warned her to steer clear, because he sensed the guy was dangerous.

But Tangie's jewelry collection was growing by the week and all with just the *promise* that one day she'd let him sleep with her. But Vega became impatient and more aggressive until he was banned from the club.

She had a small apartment a few blocks from the club, so most nights she just walked, because even though the club had security, theft still occurred and she did not want to put her uninsured Lexus on the lot.

The first week after he was banned, Tangie was careful, watching around her as she walked home, knowing Vega might try something. But when almost a month went by without incident she let her guard down.

And that's when he attacked.

Even five years later, Mikayla could still feel the pain as he shoved a knife into her ribs and beat her in the face with his fist. She could still feel the intense fear as she believed her life was about to end. She could still feel the terror as he forced her to the ground and tried to rape her.

Then there were these sounds around her as Vega fell back off her. Through her swollen eyes she could not make out what was happening, but the sounds eventually became distinguishable. There was the snarling and growling of a dog, chaos and commotion as the man and dog fought. Vega's shouts of pain as the dog bit into his legs, his arms any part of the man she could reach. A heartbreaking yelp of pain as Vega managed to slice the dog with the knife. The sounds of Vega trying to get away. Mikayla thought the dog would follow and finish him off, but instead she stayed with Mikayla, barking her displeasure at the man's retreating back. And then the silence.

Mikayla could hear the dog's claws against the concrete as she paced. Her furry head nudged Mikayla until she moved. Seeming satisfied she was still alive, the dog continued her pacing, and Mikayla struggled to hold on to consciousness.

Later she would be told the attack lasted a few minutes, but to Mikayla those moments seemed an eternity. It may have been a few minutes but it was long enough to change her whole life.

While they waited for help, the dog would pace a while, then sit with her a while, and then pace some more. Mikayla thought this beast that came to her rescue would be the last thing she saw so she shared her soul's confession.

Mikayla talked to her about how she resented her parents and her entire childhood. She told her about the warning Nisha had given her and how she wished she would've listened. She told her about how stripping had started out as fun, but somewhere she'd lost control of the game. And she told her about her dreams. Of how she'd always loved writing and if she managed to get out of this situation she would write. She even promised the mutt a home.

The nervous dog seemed to almost listen at times, but most of her attention was focused on the street, watching and waiting. When she thought she could not hold on any longer Mikayla surrendered to the heavy weight of a deep sleep.

It was almost three months before she became conscious of anything around her. Not awake exactly, it was more like a waking dream.

She heard the nurses discussing her situation right over her bed as if she were not there. They spoke of how she'd been downgraded from hospital to hospice because it was believed she had a short while to live.

The nurse spoke of a dog that had started hanging around outside the small hospice, much to the staff's concern because she had blood caked in her fur. At first, Mikayla could not believe it was the same dog, but when she heard her familiar whimpering outside her first-floor window she knew it was.

Then something changed. She wasn't sure if it were her concern for the dog that awakened her or the natural healing process. She only knew she was frightened of what would become of her protector.

She tried to tell the nurses how the dog had rescued her, but they showed little sympathy and attempted to have the dog picked up by animal control more than once. But the animal was smarter than they gave her credit for, disappearing before the truck arrived and returning when the coast was clear.

Meanwhile, Mikayla found out while she'd been hospitalized for three months, she'd lost her apartment and all her belongings and her Lexus had been re-possessed.

Mikayla felt hopeless and helpless to do anything about the situation. Sensing her anxiety a volunteer had suggested she start a journal. Within a few days she'd filled several journal notebooks, spilling out all her thoughts and feelings and finding the process to be cathartic.

By the time she'd finished her journals she was looking at the eviction as a chance to start over. After all, the apartment and everything in it had belonged to Tangie, and Tangie no longer existed.

Mikayla began feeling better by the day. Her only sadness being she had no way to protect the animal that had fought so hard to protect her. The dog would disappear, sometimes for days at a time, but she always returned, and Mikayla was certain the animal control people would catch her and possibly euthanize her if they felt she was dangerous.

After rereading her journals several times, Mikayla got an idea. When she was healthy enough to walk, she began using the hospice library computer to organize her journals into a book. It took her almost a month, but finally it was ready to send off.

She found a literary agency in Florida and used the only return address she had, the hospice. Even as she asked a nurse to postmark it for her, Mikayla had decided the outcome didn't matter. Regardless of whether it was published or not, just the sense of accomplishment was enough.

She was startled when an agent from the firm, Kandi Martin, showed up at the hospice unannounced. The woman had been intrigued by not only the book itself, but the return address of the writer. She'd come expecting to find someone on their deathbed, and instead found a woman on the road to recovery.

Mikayla had labeled the story fiction, but Kandi had known the moment she read it that it was based on real experiences and no matter how she tried to talk Mikayla into changing the category, she refused.

But she did open up to Kandi and explain the circumstances that had brought her to this place in her life, including the dog that rescued her. The two women came to a sort of strange agreement, one that included Kandi taking custody of the dog until Mikayla could get up on her feet.

Six months from the day of her attack, Mikayla purchased a new car. A small Chevy sedan and a far cry from her Lexus. And a week later, she had packed what few possessions she owned, her scruffy companion she'd christened "Angel," and headed for Miami where Kandi lived, never looking back.

Over the past five years, she'd built a good life for herself, but had found there were side effects of the attack. She became more and more of a recluse until she'd cut off all contact with the outside world, except for Kandi.

That was when Kandi suggested the seminars. Reluctantly, Mikayla agreed to do one, and stumbled into her calling when she looked out over the faces of that first group of women, knowing each of those lives contained stories of pain and broken hearts. Somehow her book had brought them together, and now they were looking to her for words of healing. In that moment, she understood why everything had happened. It was so that the arrogant, selfish young woman she'd started out as could become the woman she was today.

As she pulled up in front of the conference center in Fort Lauderdale forty minutes later, Mikayla felt emotionally drained. She tried not to think back to that time in her life often, because even now the pain was too sharp. But she understood that sometimes looking back was necessary to see how far you'd come. And she had come so far.

Mikayla was very proud of the way she'd recovered from her attack, and turned her life around. The exotic dancer known as Tangie was dead. Mikayla had killed her the same night Vega had tried to take her life. That night, she'd been reborn into Mikayla Shroeder, Christian inspirational author and motivational speaker.

So much had changed in her life since that fateful night. The girl she once was would not even recognize the woman she'd become. That girl was careless, arrogant and selfish and it had cost her more than she ever dreamed possible.

But over the years, she'd become stronger, tougher than she ever imagined she could be. She grabbed her attaché and hopped out of the car. Seeing Dusty's face before her once more, she shook away the image. It had been a long time since she'd been vulnerable to anyone, and she wasn't about to start now.

Chapter 6

Dusty stood across the play yard from his nemesis—and over the past two weeks she had indeed become his nemesis. "You think you're so smart, don't you?"

She looked back with bright eyes and a wagging tail.

"You don't even have opposable thumbs."

Angel didn't seem the slightest bit put off by the rebuke. Her tail continued to wag. She seemed content to play another round of their little game called try-to-put-a-leash-on-me.

Dusty sighed in frustration. Mikayla was scheduled to arrive any minute and he had nothing to show for the past two weeks of training. Angel had resisted his reconditioning at every turn.

Not only had she resisted retraining, she'd begun to be a nuisance throughout the entire ranch. Almost every day she found a new way out of the play pen and he would get reports from the hospital that she was inciting the other animals, or from the stables, where she could chase the horses.

The reason he did not keep her locked up inside was that he'd told Mikayla he wouldn't. Since the first day when she'd so peacefully allowed them to leash her collar, not a single trainer including Dusty had been able to get the leash on her again.

With most of the trainers, save Sam, she was outright aggressive. But she saved her special tricks for Dusty.

It started early in the morning on her second day on the ranch. Dusty had come to pick her up to begin her training. When he moved toward her kennel, she simply watched him, and when he opened the door of her pen she made no attempt to exit.

Taking it as a good sign, Dusty bent inside the pen to hook the leash onto her collar, and that's when he heard it. A low, deep rumble coming from her chest.

Dusty backed out of the pen. After a lifetime of working with dogs he knew a warning growl when he heard it. But as he looked at her face, nothing had changed in her expression. She was still watching him.

He thought maybe he'd imagined the growl until he moved toward her and heard it again. Dusty sat back on his heels and looked at the dog. There was nothing about her demeanor indicating threatening behavior, except the growl.

He glanced up at Sam, the trainer he'd assigned to help him with Angel. The man was standing right beside him. "Did you hear that?"

Sam frowned. "Hear what?"

"She growled at me."

Sam looked at the dog and then at Dusty with a strange expression. "No, I didn't hear anything."

Dusty moved toward her again, and all was fine until he reached up to put the leash on her collar and the low, rumbling growl reverberated through her body and the small pen.

Dusty backed up and got to his feet. He looked at Angel, who was still sitting, waiting. Then she wagged her tail and gave a loud, happy bark.

"You okay, Dusty?" Sam asked, seeing the expression on his face.

"I keep hearing a deep-throated growl whenever I get close to her." He handed the leash to Sam. "Here, you try it."

Sam shrugged and kneeled before the pen. Dusty watched, annoyed as Sam hooked the leash onto the dog's collar without so much as a murmur from the dog.

Dusty frowned as he watched Sam lead Angel out of her pen. "Has she been experiencing any pain lately?"

Sam glanced at him with a confused expression. "No, as a matter of fact, I expected some anxiety from her being here on her first night. But instead, she slept like a baby."

"Hmm." Dusty moved toward the dog when, without warning, she snapped at him.

Dusty jumped back and Sam's eyes widened in surprise. "Wow, I've never seen anything like that before," Sam said, tightening his hold on the leash.

Dusty knew exactly what he was talking about. It was the fact that nothing in Angel's stance or attitude had indicated her displeasure. Most dogs—in fact, every dog he'd ever interacted with—gave warning signs in their demeanor. Dusty was a firm believer that anyone who was ever attacked by a dog and expressed surprise at the attack was someone who just wasn't paying attention.

Dusty's eyes narrowed. "I wonder, does she have a history of aggressive behavior?"

"Did you ask the owner?"

Dusty ignored the question. He was too embarrassed to mention he was so caught up in Mikayla Shroeder's perfect-fitting jeans that he'd asked very few questions. And thanks to Angel's stunt of running off with Hannah's dress, the paperwork had not even been completed. Dusty had planned to ask Mikayla to finish it today.

Dusty glanced at the dog and was once again amazed to see nothing in her body language that indicated anger or aggression. She sat on the floor with her tongue lolling to the side, looking up at him.

He'd never seen a dog who gave no indication of its emotional state before an attack. It was almost as if he was dealing with two different dogs—both of which were dangerous.

He decided to let Sam work with her most of the day until he could better understand why she was okay with him one day and different the next.

The next morning the same thing happened, but instead of letting Sam take her, Dusty decided to try to lure her out with milk bones. She took the treat, but since the hairs on the back of his neck were still standing, Dusty decided not to get too close.

Angel allowed him to put the leash on her collar, but Dusty was already considering what to tell Mikayla.

Based on her behavior, some part of him believed she was dangerous and unstable. But the look of pain in Mikayla's eyes told him she loved the mangy mutt, and from the way the dog sat looking up at her adoringly, the feeling was mutual.

Angel tilted her head to the side, as her eyes glanced between his face and the hand that contained the milk bones. She started forward and then stopped, looking up at Sam. After a while, she sat back down and ignored the milk bone.

Prideful thing. Dusty made a ticking sound, and continued to coo and coax, and he could see Angel was torn between her image and taking the offered milk bone.

He started making the cooing sound once more, and this time Angel paused before moving across the floor to collect the biscuit. Sniffing at the offered hand, she scooped up the biscuit and in two bites it was gone. While the dog ate, Dusty took the opportunity to check for bumps or physical injuries, still trying to find the cause of her initial reaction to him.

"Everything okay?" Sam called over his shoulder.

"Yes, she seems fine."

The dog had relaxed, so Dusty led her outside. Their truce lasted until the treats were gone. And once again, Angel returned to the low, unexpected growl every time he tried to make her do something she did not want to. But as the days wore on, Dusty began to understand that despite her strange behavior, Angel was no more dangerous than any other dog.

In fact, she was less dangerous dog, and more spoiled mutt. He couldn't help wondering if she growled at

Mikayla to get her way at home. He added questions to the growing list in his brain.

After the third day, Dusty allowed Angel to remain in the yard with the other dogs to build social skills, but soon discovered what a mistake it was. Angel was a natural born leader and soon she'd replaced him as the alpha in the play yard.

Once her leadership had been established she began finding ways out of the play yard. The crawl space under the training building, digging holes under the gate—and what was most impressive was the speed with which she did it.

And no sooner would he and the other trainers round up Angel and her fellow escapees than she would be back at it again. She'd even somehow managed to recruit Athos, Porthos and Aramis into her little gang.

Frankly, he wanted the *scrappy little fur-coated headache* off his property, but that was not an option. Because along with Angel would go Mikayla. And Dusty was nowhere near ready to say goodbye to her.

From the moment she drove away from the ranch two weeks ago, she had been all he could think about. He'd gone online to find out what he could about her and discovered the most important fact. She was single.

He dug around his house until he found her book and reread it. She wrote in third person, but it was obvious some of it was based on her own experiences. The emotion was simply too raw to be completely fictional.

He'd counted the days waiting for her to return for her two-week visit, but now that it was here, he was hoping she would not show. Because he had nothing to offer in the way of improved behavior.

As he and Angel stood facing off in the yard, the small form of a woman coming from the direction of the hospital appeared.

Dusty relaxed his stance and was surprised to see Angel do the same. He slowly sat down on the ground. Once he was seated on the ground, Angel loped over to him and licked his face in satisfaction.

It came to Dusty like an epiphany. The problem between them wasn't *her* inability to be trained, Dusty realized. It was *his*.

There could be one pack leader, and Angel had decided that leader would be her. Which meant Dusty would have to heel.

He rubbed her under her chin. "Like hell," he said in a singsong voice. "You listen here, you mangy mutt," he continued in the playful voice. "I'm the alpha around here and you best not forget it." He rubbed her belly. "But if this is what it will take to get through this afternoon without Mikayla knowing what a hopeless case you are, so be it." He rubbed behind her ears. "But tomorrow is a new day and a new way." His voice never changed from the playful, baby cooing. "Yes, it is. Yes, it is."

Just then Mikayla reached the gate. "Angel!"

At the sound of her name, the dog's floppy ears perked up and she turned toward the sound. Spotting Mikayla, she raced to the fence and attempted to poke her nose through the open holes, trying to lick any part of her she could reach.

Mikayla turned from the gate and rushed into the building and out into the play yard, and Angel was right at the door to meet her. As Dusty watched the reunion, his resolve to train Angel was strengthened.

Regardless of the whys, it was obvious Mikayla loved the dog, and for that reason alone he wanted to give her the obedient pet she deserved. He stood and dusted his jeans as he came over to them.

Today, she looked professional in a navy blue pants suit that was getting covered in dirt. Her long hair was twisted up in a loose bun, and she wore a touch of makeup, which he knew from her last visit she did not need.

She looked up at him and smiled. "I had no idea how much I would miss her."

"As you can see, she has missed you, too."

"Look what I have!" She pulled a stuffed toy from her pocket and tossed it, and Angel took off after it. Mikayla looked up at Dusty with a resolved expression, and he realized in that moment she was expecting bad news. "How did she do?"

He smiled. "Not bad. Kind of a rocky start. But it goes like that sometimes. We'll figure each other out eventually."

Her eyes widened. "So, you're not sending her home?"

"Why would I do that?"

"Well, other trainers have given up after one afternoon with her, and she's been here two full weeks."

"I told you before I haven't met a dog I couldn't train, and that still stands."

"Oh." A look of disappointment came over her face. "That's great."

Dusty laughed. "I can tell you're real pleased."

"I am." She shrugged. "You *really are* our last chance. I just miss her, that's all."

"Not sure I like being seen as a last chance. But don't worry, I'm sure these weeks will fly by in no time."

Mikayla watched Angel toss her favorite stuffed toy, swinging it in every direction. "She seems happy." She glanced around the play area. "Where are the other dogs?"

"We've found it better to work with Angel without distraction."

She frowned. "Oh. I hope you're not making them stay in their pens all day to accommodate us."

"Oh—not at all. We work with them one-on-one for two hours of the day and then we work with them as a group."

"Oh." She yawned, and only then did Dusty notice the dark bags under her eyes.

"How have you been?" he asked.

"Pretty good—a little tired, though. I just did a seminar in Fort Lauderdale."

"Oh, really? What kind of seminar?"

"Self-empowerment for women."

"I did notice your book had a somewhat female bias."

She gave him a hard look. "What's that supposed to mean?"

Dusty's eyes widened at the tone of her voice. "Nothing, just you see things from a woman's point of view, which is perfectly natural."

She studied his face for a few seconds, and then turned back to gesture Angel over. The dog loped across the yard to her for a brief moment before taking off again.

"Sorry, I'm touchy about that particular subject. I've been called everything from a man-hater to a lesbian, all thrown out as slurs."

Dusty frowned in surprise. "I'm sorry. I didn't know."

She shrugged. "It's okay. I'm used to it. The seminars always wear me out, but I couldn't go home without seeing my baby."

Angel had retreated to the other side of the yard, and she was busy rooting around in the grass.

Dusty and Mikayla stood watching her for a few minutes before Mikayla said, "I better get going. Long ride back to the city."

Dusty knew it was now or never. "Um, Mikayla, I was wondering if you'd like to have dinner with me sometime?"

She paused, and glanced at him nervously. "I'm flattered, but—"

He held up a hand. "It's okay. I just thought I would ask."

The pair stood in an awkward silence for several seconds before Mikayla said, "So…about the training sessions."

Dusty nodded. "Right. Can you start tomorrow?"

"I sure can."

"We like to have the dog and owner work together two to three times a week. Will you be able to fit that into your schedule?"

"I'll fit whatever I have to into my schedule. Like I told you, Angel is very important to me."

"Okay, then. I guess we'll see you tomorrow. Is nine too early?"

"No, I'll be here, nine o'clock."

Another awkward silence fell over them, and Dusty had that strange sensation of experiencing her emotions. Today it was a thin layer of nervousness in the air.

Mikayla thought about calling to Angel once more, but she was having so much fun playing with her toy she decided not to. Besides, she would be seeing her in the morning anyway. "Well, good night." She turned and headed back to her car.

"Good night," Dusty called after her, and as soon as she was gone so was the oppressive air. He shook his head. "Weird."

Just then, Steve came out of the building to take Angel for a walk. "What's weird?" he asked.

Dusty turned in surprise, not hearing his employee walk up. "Nothing." He glanced at Angel who was still happily playing, not even noticing that Mikayla was gone.

Dusty wondered briefly if maybe his radar was off. He would've sworn that he was getting a vibe from Mikayla. More than just that freaky strong emotion thing she seemed to generate, but a genuine woman-into-man kind of vibe. Of course, it was entirely possible that he read her wrong. After all he knew very little about her. She could be in a relationship for all he knew. Mikayla Shroeder excited every nerve in his body by simply standing next to him, but if he didn't do it for her that was just something he would have to accept.

Chapter 7

It took Dusty less than a week of working with Mikayla in close quarters to confirm his suspicion. It was a suspicion that had begun the day he took her to meet his dogs. It was a suspicion that made him want to kill a man.

At some point in her life someone had hurt her.

The evidence was in the way she flinched every time they accidentally brushed against one another. It was in the way she watched his every move, always on guard. She smiled, she joked with him, but all it took was one look in her eyes to know she did not trust him.

With each passing day he grew more and more frustrated by his inability to help her. Not that he had any idea how to.

Some days they sat in his office and talked about her relationship with the dog, but other days they worked side by side, training Angel, which meant sometimes their bodies made contact and each and every time it happened she stiffened up like an ironing board.

That only increased his frustration because the more he learned about her, the more he wanted to know.

"Where's Angel?" Mikayla looked around the large, open room where she'd just arrived. Most mornings, Angel was there to greet her. But that morning she and Dusty were the only occupants.

"We'll bring her in later, but for now. I want to work with just you."

"What do you mean?"

"Dogs learn about us from out body language, and yours screams walk-all-over-me."

She straightened her shoulders. "I don't think so."

"Good, that's good. But that's not your normal posture."

He crossed behind her and went to reach for her shoulders and Mikayla quickly turned and moved away from him. "What are you doing?"

"I just wanted to show you the correct way to stand."

Her lips firmed as her eyes darted to his hands. "Can't you just tell me?"

Dusty looked into her eyes for a moment and nodded. "Okay." He straightened his own posture. "Angel has become the alpha in your relationship because you were not being the alpha. Now you have to take that status back." He gestured to his body. "It's all about confidence."

Mikayla tried to imitate his pose, and instinctively Dusty moved to correct her body. And once again she backed away from him.

"I see what you mean," she said, struggling to strike just the right pose.

"Okay, now remember when you walk her, *you* lead. *You* decide where you want to go."

"I already do that."

"Really?"

She nodded.

"Sam, can you take Angel out?" he called over his shoulder.

As Sam walked the dog through the room leading to the outside door, she saw Mikayla and became excited, tugging at the leash struggling to get to her.

Mikayla automatically hunched over and moved to greet the dog.

"Wrong," Dusty said with a shake of his head. "Look at what you're doing."

"What? I'm greeting my dog," she said, rubbing Angel's furry chin.

"No, you're surrendering to her." He crossed the room to her, and taking her waist stood her straight again. Dusty could feel her whole body stiffen in his hands, and the storm clouds began to roll in. He immediately let her go and just as quickly felt her relax.

Sam led Angel through the door leading to the outdoor play area. Mikayla glanced at Dusty nervously, and quickly looked away. "How is greeting her surrendering?"

"It's not the *what,* it's the *how.*" He imitated her hunched-over position. "See?"

Mikayla frowned. "I don't look like that."

He stood straight up. "Actually, you do."

"Well, I guess it's better than that pimp walk you have going on." She laughed.

His eyes narrowed menacingly, but the slight upturn of his mouth belied the seriousness. "*Pimp* walk?"

"Yeah, that thing you do…" She began imitating walking around the room, leaning to one side.

Dusty laughed out loud. "You look like a crab."

Mikayla paused in her imitation. "Hmm, now that you mention it, I think a crab would be an apt description of the way you walk."

"Well, crab or not, my dogs respect me, and if you want Angel's respect you're going to have to stop going *to her* all the time." He winked. "Show her who's boss."

Mikayla sighed. "I'm afraid she already knows."

"Hungry?" Dusty asked, heading into his office. He came back out carrying a picnic basket.

"What's that?"

He held up the basket. "I packed a lunch for us this morning, more than plenty enough for two."

"That's very thoughtful." She followed him back into the office.

Dusty cleared a space on the small conference table he used for staff meetings and set the basket down. Soon the pair were tearing through a light lunch of assorted miniature sandwiches and bottled water, along with Chex Mix and Suzy-Q's.

"So, tell me," Dusty asked toying with one of the sandwiches, "why aren't you seeing anyone?"

Mikayla glanced up quickly, and then looked away. But it was not before he saw the wariness in her eyes or felt it in the air.

"I'm sorry," he said, focusing his attention on his sandwich. "I had no right to ask such a personal question."

She smiled. "I could ask the same of you."

He gestured around them. "The job."

She smirked. "You mean, the *passion*. You love your job—anyone can see that."

"I won't deny it." He nodded. "I do take a certain amount of pride in it."

"It's only natural to love something you worked hard to build."

They continued to nibble on their sandwiches and eat in quiet. Dusty asked, "What inspired you to write your book?"

"There just seemed like a lot of women out there who could use some uplifting."

"Have you always been a spiritual person?"

She paused for a long moment. "No, not exactly."

"Well, I must admit that when I found out who you were I was a bit intimidated."

"Why?" She frowned.

"I'm not nearly as strong in my faith as you are. I mean, that chapter on living the good life…wow." He shook his head. "That takes some serious fortitude."

Mikayla said nothing, just continued to eat. A quiet settled over the pair and Dusty wondered if she was uncomfortable talking about herself.

After a while she tossed her paper plate with the remnants of a small sandwich in the trash and stood, dusting her hands. "Well, thank you for the lunch."

He smiled back. "Thank you for the company."

After that day, Dusty made sure he always brought

a picnic basket on the days Mikayla was scheduled to be there, and each time they spent a portion of the day sitting and talking and eating.

Over the course of the next week, Dusty began to see signs of progress. The flinching whenever they accidentally bumped into each other had stopped. And he found he could even touch her deliberately without a bad reaction.

It was after one of the days when Angel, feeling generous, did exactly as she was told and everything could not have gone more perfect that Dusty decided to try to ask Mikayla out again.

It was just starting to get dark as he was walking her back to her car. "Mikayla, I have a couple of tickets to a fundraiser in a month and I was hoping you would go with me."

"What kind of fundraiser?"

He frowned. "Marine life protection, I think."

"I *think?*"

He shrugged. "I support so many of these things I can't keep track. Normally, I don't even bother going to these kinds of things, but—"

"Sure. I would love to."

They walked on in silence, but Dusty was feeling like the luckiest man in the world. And although he should've known better, he decided to try to push his luck.

They reached her car and he turned to face her. "Actually, I don't want to wait a month to go out with you. Can we go out to dinner sometime?"

She laughed, but it did not reach her eyes. "You don't play around, do you?" She shrugged. "Okay, when?"

"How about tomorrow—if that's not too soon?"

She laughed out loud. "No, no tomorrow sounds great. Should I meet you somewhere?"

"I can pick you up at your place, if you like."

Something flashed across her face. "Why don't we just meet somewhere this time?"

Dusty knew she was taking the necessary precautions of any single woman living alone, but he so wanted to tell her she had nothing to fear from him. "Okay, how about Delmonico's at eight-thirty?"

She frowned. "Delmonico's? I heard the waiting list is two months long."

He smiled. "Don't worry, we'll get in. So, Delmonico's at eight-thirty?"

Chapter 8

"A circus—really?" Mikayla twirled her pasta on her fork as she listened to Dusty describe his unconventional childhood.

"That's where I first fell in love with animals." She watched as his handsome face took on a sad expression. "Not all circuses treated their animals the way they should. My father was always emphatic about that. No one in our group would ever mistreat animals."

"I know what you mean. I saw a documentary once about how some circus animals are treated."

"Unfortunately, it's true about some, but not all circuses mistreat their animals, and yet they all get painted with the same brush." He cut into his steak and glanced across the table at her. "What about you?"

She shrugged. "Nothing as interesting as the circus. Just your typical childhood." She sipped at the wine and Dusty waited for her to continue, but she didn't.

He wondered if she'd been vague on purpose, or did she consider her childhood so insignificant?

"Does your father still own the circus?" she asked.

Dusty nodded. "Yes, and I think he always will. He loves the life."

"And you don't?"

"No, I do not. Don't get me wrong, it's not a bad life, just wasn't the life for me. I wanted something more stable, one place I could call home. A place I could raise a family someday."

She laughed. "Well, you definitely have enough room to raise a family."

Dusty was lifting a forkful of asparagus to his mouth and he paused. In the short time he'd known her he'd seen her soft smile, and the hints of laughter, but to see her face in full bloom…she was even more beautiful than he'd originally thought.

She glanced away, and he realized his staring was making her nervous. "So, what made you want to write a book?"

"The usual, I guess. I think we all experience things and believe what we learned could benefit someone else. I decided to test that theory."

"Considering your success, I would say you were right."

"Thank goodness." She leaned across the table. "Not sure what I would've done if the book had flopped."

There it was again, Dusty thought, cutting off another bite of his steak. Deliberate vagueness. He wasn't sure if it were the result of it being their first date, and she was still unsure about him, or if she was simply guarded.

"Okay, I gotta ask. Where did you find Angel?"

Mikayla's expression took on a faraway look. "I didn't. She found me." She looked at him. "At a time when I could use a friend, she just appeared out of nowhere."

"So you just took her home?"

"Something like that."

"What if she'd belonged to someone else?"

"It was pretty obvious she was a stray."

"Hmm." He cut the steak and popped another bite into his mouth. When he looked up again, she was frowning at him.

"What does *hmm* mean?"

"What are you talking about?"

"When I said Angel was a stray, you said 'hmm.'"

"I don't think so." He shook his head.

"Um, yeah, you did."

He shrugged. "If I did, I apologize. I meant nothing by it."

That seemed to appease her and she returned her attention to her meal. Dusty watched her eat for a few moments, growing more and more peeved he had to apologize for making a noise.

"You know, on second thought, I did mean something by it."

She looked up at him again.

"Do I make you nervous?"

She frowned. "No. Why would you think that?"

"Well, our conversation. I've been talking to you for over an hour and I still don't know anything about you."

"Of course you do. We've discussed our upbringing, our—"

"Correction. I discussed my upbringing. Life as

a carnie kid. You just said something about typical childhood, whatever that means. I told you specifically why I got into veterinarian science, and all you said was that you wrote *for the usual reasons*."

He shrugged in confusion. "I may be wrong, but it seems to me as if you are deliberately saying little about yourself. Is it because I make you nervous?"

Her mouth twisted in obvious annoyance. "You don't make me nervous, Dusty."

"Then what is it?"

She glanced around the restaurant at the people dining around them. Each table seemed deep in their own discussion, and Dusty was almost certain she was stalling.

She looked directly at him. "Dusty, I haven't done this in a while."

"Done what?"

She gestured to the table. "This." She nodded toward him. "You."

He frowned as understanding began to sink in. "Do you mean date? You haven't dated in a while?"

"Exactly. So, my *technique* may be a bit rusty. I spend most of my time with Angel, and as much as I love her, she is not the most stimulating conversationalist."

Dusty laughed. "I see your point." He reached across the table and took her hand in his. "But I just don't want you thinking you have to hide things from me. I know you just met me, but believe me when I say I would never hurt you."

"I believe you," she whispered.

"Good. I'm glad that's out of the way." He turned his attention back to his steak.

For the next two hours they continued to have the one-sided conversation with Dusty sharing and Mikayla dodging questions like a spy.

But despite the awkward conversation the evening was still one of the most enjoyable he'd experienced in a long time and he did not want it to come to an end.

As he walked her to her car, Dusty took her by the elbow and stopped her. "I had a great time tonight."

"Me, too."

"Can I see you again?"

She seemed to hesitate, and for a moment Dusty thought she would say no, and then she nodded yes. "I would like that very much."

He moved closer to her, so as not to frighten her. He'd been thinking about kissing her all night, and now that the time was here he was cautioning himself to take it slow. She was already as jumpy as a rabbit. One false move and she would bolt.

She let him slip his arms around her waist and pull her closer, even though she held her body stiff in his arms. He brought his face closer to hers, giving her time to get used to the feel of his hands on her body. Giving her time to get used to him being this close.

Then when she did nothing to resist, he pressed his lips to hers and released a floodgate of passion. It was as if with just the touching of their lips, he'd awakened sleeping beauty.

Her arms slipped up and around his neck and she pulled him closer. Her mouth opened beneath his and Dusty took the invitation, plunging his tongue deep inside. Soon his hands were running over her lush hips and slender waist, touching all the wonderful curves and valleys he'd wanted to touch since the first moment he saw her running through his hospital.

"No—stop!" Dusty was so submerged in her sweet scent and taste he did not hear her, until she suddenly pushed hard against his chest and backed away. "No!" Her brown eyes were wide and frightened.

Dusty moved forward to comfort her, but stopped himself when he realized what he was doing. "What's wrong?"

"Let's...let's take it slow, okay?" she said in a trembling voice.

Dusty could see the fear in her eyes rapidly dissipating, but he knew better than most how easily it could return. He nodded. "All right, whatever you want to do."

She frowned as if wanting to say something more, but held her tongue. The pair stood staring at each other for a long time before the laughter of a group as they left the restaurant was enough to shatter the spell.

Mikayla was the first to look away. "I better get going."

"Mikayla." He paused, wondering if maybe she would consider this moving too fast, but decided to speak his mind anyway. "I'm serious here. I mean, I'm not looking for some fling. I really like you."

She bit her bottom lip as if contemplating something. "I like you, too, Dusty. I do. But...this is our first date. I don't want you to—"

"I know." He nodded. "I just wanted you to know where I'm coming from."

"Like I told you in the restaurant, I don't do this all the time. So, let's just take it slow."

"I get it. Like I said, I just don't want any confusion between us. Okay?"

She smiled up at him. "Okay. And take care of my baby. I miss her."

"She's in good hands."

"I know." She closed the door and, waving at him through the window, pulled out of the restaurant's driveway.

Dusty walked over to where his car was waiting and climbed in. As he was driving back to the ranch, he wondered to himself if maybe he should not have said how he was feeling.

He decided that regardless of whatever came next, he'd done the right thing. He wasn't sure how she felt, but he was certain he was not interested in playing games with Mikayla. It would be for real or not at all.

Every once in a while, a man met a woman he knew could change his world for better or worse. Mikayla was that kind of woman.

Chapter 9

The next few days seems like a lifetime in paradise to Mikayla. Dusty was proving to be just the man she thought he was. Patient and compassionate. Warm and wonderful, and she was finding it harder and harder to resist his charms.

More importantly, he was making her feel like herself again. For the past five years she'd been terrified at the idea of even being alone with a man for too long, but she felt nothing but safe in Dusty's presence no matter how long they were together.

It had been so long since any man had made her feel the way Dusty did with just a touch. She knew right away this was a man who could get inside her fortress. The fortress it had taken her years to build.

Every time she told him she had not experienced something, he would take it upon himself to make sure she did. Like the Indian food he'd brought over for dinner the other night after she admitted having never tasted curry.

Or the trip they had taken that morning to Disney World after she confessed she'd never been to an amusement park before. Like two kids they spent the entire day riding every ride and playing every game.

Now, they entered her house late in the evening. "Care for something to drink?"

"Thanks," he said, his eyes taking in her décor. "But I don't drink alcohol. Got any soda?"

"One ginger ale coming right up." She headed into the kitchen.

"Nice place you have here," he called after her.

"Thanks."

She grabbed two bottles of ginger ale and glasses and headed back into the living room. "Here you go."

Dusty waited until she sat down beside him, before he said, "No pictures of family?"

Mikayla glanced around the room as if noticing this startling fact for the first time. "Hmm, never noticed. Guess I'll have to fix that. You know I haven't been in the house very long."

"I thought you said you'd been here a year."

She forced a laugh. "That's what I mean by not very long." She reached over to the table and opened his ginger ale bottle and poured some into a glass. "There you go."

When she looked up at him again, Dusty was just watching her.

She smiled. "What?"

"You have the strongest emotions I've ever seen."

"What do you mean?"

He shook his head in confusion. "I think if I tried to explain it, it wouldn't make sense."

Mikayla stared back with her own confusion for a moment before opening her own bottle of ginger ale and drinking it straight out of the bottle. "Thank you for today, by the way. It was wonderful."

"My pleasure. I had a great time, as well." He looked at her and found her soft brown eyes studying his face. "You have any idea how beautiful you are?"

Instead of the compliment bringing a bright smile to her face, it seemed to sadden her a bit.

"Thank you," she said softly.

And Dusty added one more facet to the complex personality of Mikayla Shroeder.

She reached over and placed her hand on top of his, and Dusty realized it was the first time she'd deliberately touched him. "Coming from you that means something, so really—thank you."

He looked down at where her hand covered his and felt he was experiencing the most intimate moment of his life. "You're welcome." Dusty watched in fascination as her index finger slowly began to trace over his hand. When his eyes came back up to meet hers he was stunned by what he saw there. Flagrant desire.

Slowly he leaned in to kiss her, and she pulled back briefly before leaning forward again.

Dusty leaned back and looked into her eyes. "Don't do anything you're not comfortable with, Mikayla."

She looked deep into his eyes for several long seconds before she leaned forward and touched her lips to his.

Dusty wanted to reach out to her, to take her into his arms, but he was afraid it would scare her off. She had initiated this kiss, and even if it killed him, he would allow her to decide how far it would go.

Her soft lips pressed harder against his, and he released a slight groan, feeling her soft, wet tongue dart out, searching. On a heavy sigh, Dusty opened his mouth and let her take her exploration to the next level, and she did.

She scooted across the sofa until she was closer to him and put her arms around his neck. Dusty's hands were itching to take her into his arms, but instead he balled his hands into fists to keep them off her.

Tilting her head to the side, she opened her mouth over his and the kiss deepened. Dusty felt his erection growing in his pants and wondered if she had any idea what she was doing with a simple kiss.

Just when he thought he could not take anymore, she drew back, leaving him with one final soft touch of their lips. Slowly Dusty opened his eyes and saw that she had scooted back to the other side of the sofa, but there was something different about her.

There was a sparkle in her eyes, and she was smiling at him. Dusty swallowed hard and knew that he had met his limitation for the night. He stood. "Well, it's late, I better get going."

Mikayla stood with him, and as he moved toward the door she stepped into his path and wrapped her arms around his neck pressing her body to his. Unable to stop himself, Dusty felt his arms go around her, but the sweet embrace was over as quickly as it began as she once again stepped back.

On the drive home, Dusty kept thinking about the kiss, and wondering what it meant. He had no idea what had happened to Mikayla, but he suspected it was physical abuse at the hands of a man. Maybe an old boyfriend.

Whatever the case may be, he was almost certain he was handling it properly by allowing Mikayla to set the pace. Wherever their relationship went after tonight would be completely up to her.

It wasn't long before Dusty began to reap the fruit of his wisdom. After that evening, Mikayla became much more expressive in her affection. She started touching him more and more. Often she would just walk up to him, wrap her arms around him and kiss him. There were times when she would simply run her hands over his chest or cup his chin in her hands and just study his face.

Although her random affection was wonderful, it was also killing him because he was never certain when—if ever—they would take it to the next level, and he was dying to make love to her.

But if there was one thing Dusty had learned about Mikayla, it was that she was a kaleidoscope of complex emotions and he wanted nothing more than all the time in the world to try to unravel them all.

Chapter 10

Dusty found himself thinking about Mikayla all the time. At home. At work. He could not get his mind off of her. He kept replaying the images over and over in his head. The way she touched him, the way she looked at him with the raw desire written right there in her eyes. Her sweet kisses were more perfect than anything he could've ever imagined. And yet...she was still holding back.

A soft knock on his office door brought him out of his contemplation. "Come in."

Hannah poked her head around the door, and held up a few envelopes.

"Great, thanks, Hannah." He motioned for her to bring him the mail. After she left, he put aside the X-rays he'd been reviewing and looked over the stack of mail.

A letter with familiar handwriting and no return

address caught his attention. He knew right away who it was from, and he opened the letter from his father.

Kyle Warren was what could only be described as old-school. He owned neither a cell phone or computer and rarely used the telephone. Almost all of his communications were done through letters. Dusty had often thought his father's one-man war against technology was his way of trying to preserve his gypsy lifestyle.

Dusty sat back in his chair and read:

Hi, son,

Sorry for the short notice, but I'm writing to ask a favor. The circus has fallen on hard times, and I need your help. Over the past few months we've had much smaller crowds than usual, even in the cities where we do better than average. I'm chalking it up to this bad economy of ours, but placing blame doesn't solve the problem.

As a result of this, I was not able to renew my circus/carnival license in time for our Birmingham, Alabama, performance, and the city would not allow us to set up camp. Needless to say, this setback just made matters worse.

So I'm writing to let you know we need to camp out on your ranch until I can get our license straightened out. I wouldn't inconvenience you if we had somewhere else to go, but you're the only one I know of with the room to accommodate everyone, including the animals.

We're not looking for charity. We are all more than willing to work to pay our way, and we just need a place to stay temporarily.

By the time you get this letter we will already
be heading your way, so we will arrive at the ranch
by the end of the week. See you then.
Pop

Dusty leaned forward and placed his hands over his
face. "Damn," he whispered to the empty room.

The last thing he needed right now was for his ranch
to be overrun by elephants, tigers and fire eaters. But
how could he turn them away? The motley crew that
made up the Warren Traveling Circus was the only
family he had.

Dusty stood from his chair and crossed to look out
the window that overlooked the ranch. *His* ranch. Acres
and acres of land bought and paid for by his sacrifice.

He knew a lot of men in his position would see the
open fields of green grass and tall trees as a waste of
space and money, but for Dusty it was all he'd ever
wanted: wide-open spaces. Standing there looking out
over the fields, he felt the conflicting emotions he always
felt when it came to his father and the circus.

When people asked him about his background, he
would tell them he grew up in a circus and they would
think of dancing elephants and flying trapeze artist.
They would assume growing up in a circus would be
second only to growing up in Disneyland. Most of the
time, he did nothing to dissuade that opinion.

A lifetime of training was not broken easily and from
the time he could talk he'd been taught not to speak
ill of the circus. But what no one ever considered was
what it was like after the lights went out and the people
went home. Sure they got to see dancing elephants, but

someone had to clean up after those elephants. And sure the trapeze artist performed wonderfully, with nothing but smiles and waves to the crowd below. But the crowd never realized that trapeze expert was often hiding the pain of recent injures behind those smiles. Because in the circus, hurt or not, the *show* must go on.

And not only must the show go on, but it must appear seamless to the audience. Just as a magician would never reveal his tricks to the audience, a circus master would never allow the audience to see what went on outside the big tent. And Kyle Warren was a true circus master.

But Dusty had seen it. For the first seventeen years of his life he'd lived it, without even the buffer of a mother's love. Semta Owusu had been a beautiful, equestrian rider whom Kyle had fallen head over heels in love with. But what Kyle had not realized was Semta had a wanderer's soul, and no desire to be a mother.

Kyle himself rarely talked about her. Dusty had eavesdropped on enough conversations as a child to sort out most of the story. Like the fact Semta was over her infatuation with Kyle within weeks of the love affair's beginning, but Kyle's love never died.

According to the stories he'd heard, Semta was already in the process of making preparations to leave the circus when she became aware of her pregnancy. At Kyle's request, and to honor what they'd shared, she decided to carry the child to term and give him over to Kyle to raise. Once Dusty was born and given to his father's custody, Semta disappeared from the circus and their lives forever.

Dusty had never even so much as seen a picture of her. And because carnie logic did not run the typical route, Semta had become something of a folk hero among the group. But not to Dusty.

The first several years of his life were the best memories, and he attributed that to a child's blissful ignorance. But once he was old enough to become aware of the world, the world outside the circus, he found himself longing for something different. Something that could give him a sense of stability.

Between the multitude of schools he'd attended and self teaching, Dusty had learned enough to take the test and get his GED at sixteen.

When he announced to his father he wanted to go to college, Kyle had dismissed the idea as ridiculous. But a year later when Dusty received an acceptance letter from the University of Miami, Kyle got the first glimpse of his son's rigid spine.

Dusty made it clear he was going, with or without Kyle's support, and Kyle gave in, secretly believing Dusty would miss the circus life and return. He never did.

And for several years things had been tense between the two men until a few years ago when the circus stopped in Tampa. Dusty drove up to see the show and was welcomed back into the fold by the people he'd known and loved all his life.

Now they were coming here. To *his* home.

He turned from the window and picked up the receiver on his desk phone. He dialed the number he'd already memorized and waited while it rang.

"Hello?"

"Hi, Mikayla. It's Dusty."

"Hello." The smile in her voice was all the comfort he needed.

"I was just wondering if you have any plans for lunch today?"

"As a matter of fact, I don't."

"I was thinking maybe I could grill up a couple of pork chops here and toss a salad?"

"Sounds great. What time?"

"Around twelve, if that's okay for you."

"I'll be there with fork in hand." She laughed.

By the time he hung up the phone, Dusty was feeling much better, and the cloud that had come over him after reading his father's letter had completely dissipated.

What started that afternoon with grilled pork chops continued for several days, and Dusty and Mikayla spent every available minute together. They spent the days visiting portions of the Keys neither of them had ever been to before, and their nights were spent eating at either of their homes.

Dusty was beginning to understand Mikayla's lack of details regarding her background was deliberate, and it made him more curious about the woman. Sometimes she would say or do something that made her seem so much older than her twenty-eight years, but when she was with Angel she was like a playful child.

He wasn't sure what she was hiding, but he knew it had something to do with Angel. He found himself remembering what she'd said to him on the first day. *I named her Angel for a reason.*

But despite his misgivings, he did not press her for information. He was enjoying being in her company too much to do anything that would push her away.

With each passing day, he realized his father's circus was getting closer and closer to Miami. He'd already designated a portion of the ranch for their use, and alerted his staff to the upcoming changes. At least, what changes he could warn them about.

Most of the time, when he thought about the circus, he would force away the thoughts by concentrating on something else. His work, Mikayla, anything. But sometimes the thoughts could not be pushed away, and he was left feeling a strange sense of depression he didn't quite understand.

The day before he expected his family to arrive, he and Mikayla visited Coral Castle. As they stood taking in the stone sculptures, Dusty decided to share his news with her.

"I may not be able to see you for a while."

She turned to him with a hurt expression. "Why not?"

He took a deep breath. "My father is bringing the circus here. He's having some problems with his license and needs a place to hide out. I'll be tied up with them for a while."

She smiled. "The circus is coming to town."

Dusty gave her a strange expression. "I guess you could say that."

After a few seconds of silence, she turned back to the coral sculptures, and Dusty held back the question he wanted to ask her.

Finally he gave in to the urge and just asked, "Would you like to meet them?"

She turned and hugged him, and he realized he'd just said what she wanted to hear. "I would love to."

He wrapped his arms around her and held her tight, and as it always did when he was with Mikayla the troubling feelings subsided. He was beginning to think all he needed to get through this visit was to just hold tight to Mikayla.

"Mikayla," he whispered in her ear, "I noticed you don't talk about yourself much."

She leaned back from him. "Nothing to talk about."

"I disagree. I want to know what made you."

She frowned. "What made me?"

"What things formed you into the woman you are today."

She turned back to the sculptures. "Remember what the plaque at the front of the museum said about this place?"

"What plaque?"

"It said for the thirty years he was building this place, Ed Leedskalnin refused to let anyone see him work."

"And what does that have to do with anything?"

"It also said no one is certain how he built this place, but that doesn't make it any less enjoyable to us now— does it?"

"What's your point?"

She pulled his arms close around her waist, and backed up until she was pressed against his chest. "My point is what made me, as you say, is not as important as what we have right here, right now."

Dusty stared down into her eyes and read the warning. He knew if he kept down this road he would find himself walking alone. "Okay." He nodded, deciding that for today prudence was called for. At least for today. But one day, he wanted to know the secrets she kept closed up so tight. The things she did not want to share with the world.

Before he wanted to know out of curiosity, but now, it was essential. He needed this part of her she was so reluctant to show the world as proof she cared for him as deeply as he cared for her. And he did indeed care deeply. In fact, he was falling in love.

Chapter 11

The next night, Dusty cooked dinner for Mikayla at his house. It was dusk as the pair stood over the open grill in his backyard, examining the chicken on the grill.

"I think it's ready," Mikayla said, studying the meat and listening to her stomach rumble. She'd spent the day writing, and sometimes during those periods when she was in the zone she forgot to eat. As a result, now she was starving.

Dusty shook his head. "No, not yet, just a few more minutes."

She frowned at him. "You're gonna burn it."

"I know what I'm doing." He gave her his most seductive smile. "Trust me."

"I trust you, it's my stomach that's having doubts."

Dusty closed the lid of the grill. "Just a few more minutes, and then the meat will be so tender and juicy it will fall off the bone."

"Using words like that doesn't improve matters."

His smile became a grin. "Words like what?" He walked to her and took her in his arms. "Words like... *tender*—" he slid his large hand along the outside of her thigh "—or words like *juicy*?" he whispered as his hand closed over her rounded bottom. He pulled her closer and whispered into her ear. "Those kinds of words?"

Mikayla nodded, her mind focused on the feel of his hands on her body. She reached up and wrapped her arms around his neck, pulling his mouth down to her own.

"Damn." Dusty sat her back away from him. "Stop, Mikayla." He gestured to his groin. "You're waking the beast, and if you want your dinner anytime soon, I'd advise you let him sleep."

She smiled and lifted a questioning eyebrow. "The beast? Somebody has a pretty high opinion of themselves."

He shrugged. "I'm not the one who gave it a nickname."

Her eyes narrowed to slits. "Oh, really?"

Dusty glanced at her when he realized his mistake. "I just meant—you know. Men always give their male parts outrageous nicknames. I'm sure women do it, too. For instance, what do you call her?" He gestured to her body.

"A vagina." She shook her head. "Fine, I'll leave the beast alone. Besides I'm more hungry than horny anyway." She turned back to the long picnic table where they planned to eat. "Where are your dogs?"

"Who knows." He joined her at the table. "Probably down at the circus. Ever since they arrived, I've found everyone from my staff members to nosy neighbors snooping around down there."

Mikayla glanced over her shoulder in the direction of the circus tents that could be seen even from a distance.

Seeing the forlorn expression in her eyes, Dusty said, "Don't worry, I'll take you over there soon."

"How's it been going so far?"

"Not as bad as I'd imagined. In fact, it's been kinda nice. I've seen people I haven't seen in a few years."

"And here you were worried they would take over your ranch."

"I'm still worried." He went back to check the grill, and as he lifted the lid the smoky smell floated toward Mikayla.

"Mmm, that smells wonderful."

He nodded in satisfaction. "Now it's ready."

They sat at the picnic table and ate the grilled chicken, potato salad and corn on the cob Dusty had prepared, and watched the sun set over the western edge of the property.

"It's so serene here," Mikayla said, pushing her plate away. She'd eaten until she felt ready to burst and there was still leftovers. "So peaceful."

He watched her face in the dim light. "You haven't had a lot of that, have you?"

"What? Peace?"

He nodded, still watching her emotions play across her face.

"Who has?"

"True. But there is something more going on with—"

"How's Angel?"

"What?"

"I stopped by the kennel earlier and she was not there."

"Sam has her out. She has a lot of energy for a six-year-old. He likes to take each of the dogs out for a long run in the evening."

"I guess I'll check back on the way home." She glanced at her watch. "What time do they leave for the day?"

"Six."

She frowned, glanced at her watch again and then let out a heavy sigh. "Oh, well, I guess I'll see her next time."

"Or…"

She tilted her head to the side. "Or what?"

"Or, you could stay the night and see her in the morning."

She said nothing, and for a moment Dusty regretted the suggestion.

"You're asking me to stay the night?"

"Yes."

She reached across the table and took one of his hands in hers. "Are we ready for that?"

He smiled. "I've been ready since I saw you running through my hospital." He stood from the table, and walked around to her side and held out his hand to her. "I want you, Mikayla, but I can wait. If you're not ready for this, I can wait."

Mikayla sat staring at the hand for several long

seconds before she seemed to come to some kind of decision. She bit her lip, took a deep breath and took the offered hand.

Dusty, feeling his heart pounding in his chest, led her back into the house. As they reached the back door Mikayla paused and Dusty felt as if the world had slipped out from beneath him. He turned to look at her.

"What about the food?" she asked, glancing back at the table.

Dusty felt his heart start beating again. "I'll take care of it later."

He guided her into the house and up the stairs and down the hall. He could feel Mikayla's hand going cold as he led her into his bedroom. Once they were inside, he closed the door and twisted the latch.

She looked into his eyes. "Locking us in?"

He shook his head. "No. Locking my three knuckle-heads out."

She laughed. "Do they interrupt you a lot?"

He wrapped his arms around her. "They haven't had a lot of opportunity to." Dusty took her mouth in an urgent kiss. It was as if he were a starving man, and she was a feast. As his eager hands roamed over every inch of her body, he didn't know where to start. There was so much he'd wanted to touch, to hold, to kiss, to taste. And now that she was with him, he wasn't sure he would survive the night.

Mikayla responded with an enthusiasm he'd dreamed about. She wrapped her arms around his neck and pulled him tight, parting her lips beneath his to accept his hot tongue as it explored every inch of her mouth.

Dusty wasn't sure if he'd carried her or if she'd

walked, but within seconds she was beneath him on the large, high-poster bed. His blue-jeans-clad legs pushed hers apart so he could sink into the crevice of her body.

Dusty was awed by how well their bodies fit together. It was as if she were molded just for him. But there was only one potter that could create anything as divine as Mikayla Shroeder.

He let his tongue slide over her neck in featherlight touches, savoring the shifting of her body as she tried to avoid the tickling sensation. He slid his hand between their bodies and cupped the seat of her jeans and almost groaned at the heat coming from her center. She wanted him as much as he wanted her.

Not sure he could wait much longer, Dusty sat back and pulled his polo shirt over his head, before scooping her up in his arms once more. It was as if he could not bear to stop touching her for even a moment.

Mikayla followed Dusty's lead, removing her lightweight blouse. She went to unsnap her front-latch bra, but Dusty's hand covered hers to stop her.

"Let me," he whispered in her ear.

Mikayla lay back, waiting for Dusty to remove the bra, but instead he came over the top of her, continuing to kiss her hungry mouth. He kissed her neck, her shoulder, and the tops of her breasts, working his way down to the bra.

He slipped his tongue inside, stroking her nipple beneath the satin material. His busy hand squeezed the other, exploring, and Mikayla was lost in her own body as Dusty brought it alive in ways she had not felt in years. No, in ways she'd never felt before.

As if that torment was not enough, Dusty lifted his head until he was looking at her full breast and then sucked one into his mouth with such power Mikayla arched off the bed.

Unable to wait a moment longer, Mikayla tore the bra clasp open, bearing her breasts. Her nipples stood like rigid nubs and Dusty's mouth went straight to them. He sucked first one and then the other, only to return to the first and continue the torment until Mikayla lost control.

She tore at his jeans, begging with her fingers, and Dusty obliged, slipping the jeans down his legs. Reaching into his nightstand, he found a condom and put it on.

Then Mikayla felt her own jeans being yanked down her legs along with the satin panties that matched her pink bra. Then Dusty was over the top of her, looking down into her eyes.

In that moment, Mikayla had never felt so powerful. His need was written in his eyes, it was unmistakable. And Mikayla knew she was the woman who could satisfy that need.

She parted her thighs and Dusty sank into her body. As he entered her, he released a sound that was almost pleading. Without warning, Dusty pushed up on his elbows and began plowing into Mikayla's body with the force of a madman. She matched him thrust for thrust. She didn't think she had that much passion to unleash. Mikayla held on as the tide of sexual release washed over her entire being.

Wave after wave of unrelenting pleasure washed over

her whole being until she could hold back no longer and she surrendered herself to the climax.

Feeling the change in Dusty's body, Mikayla opened her eyes just in time see his whole body go rigid and then he was flooding her with himself, and every thing he could never say with words. Mikayla held to his strong arms and accepted the tribute for what it was meant to be. The beginning....

Later, as Mikayla slept, Dusty—true to his word—went back downstairs and put away the leftovers and cleaned up their picnic. Once he was finished, he sat on the picnic table and watched the tents that were still lit up with activity in the distance.

It seemed his life had come to some kind of crossroads. So many factors were coming together. His father's arrival, his relationship with Mikayla. He was almost certain of his feelings for the woman sleeping in his bed. And if those feelings proved true, there was only one path left to take.

But as for his father, Dusty had been surprised to see the old man seemed to have slowed down. To Dusty, Kyle Warren had almost been the epitome of manhood. Strong and virile in every way. But the man he'd greeted the other day was much more frail than Dusty had known.

Dusty decided that maybe this would be the time for him and his father to make peace on certain issues. Including his mother. There was, of course, a good chance Kyle would not want such a relationship, or if he did, would not be willing to pay the price to have it.

But either way, Dusty resolved he would at least make the attempt to correct the past. A sentiment he was almost certain Mikayla understood very well.

Chapter 12

The next day, after a late lunch of cold chicken and leftover potato salad, Dusty led Mikayla from his house to the far back corner of the ranch where the circus caravan had set up camp.

Mikayla could not seem to suppress the excitement she felt.

"I can't believe you've never been to a circus," Dusty said as they walked along.

"Circuses and carnivals weren't really my family's idea of entertainment."

"I thought everyone loved the circus."

"Not everyone."

"Apparently."

"Is there a fire eater in your group?" she asked.

He smiled. "Yes, her name is Alexia. I'll introduce you."

She grinned up at him and Dusty was starting to

think maybe he should've invited his family to visit sooner.

As they came upon a crop of trees Mikayla could hear commotion and noises coming from the other side. "They're over there!" she yelled.

Dusty just looked at her with a small smile. "You know, I'm starting to get a little jealous. You never get this excited to see me."

She laughed and swung around into his arms. "Aww, don't be like that. This is a different kind of excitement."

Dusty was pleased to be the one to give it to her. "Come on." He pushed some of the trees aside and guided her through them.

Halfway through, Mikayla found herself pushing bush after bush out of her way. "Dusty?"

"Hmm." He was focused on guiding them through the thick underbrush.

"Why did you put them way back here?"

"They're a large group. They needed a lot of land."

"But this isn't land. This is a forest."

"They like their solitude."

She snatched her hand from his and stopped walking. Dusty was thrown off balance by her sudden movement and almost tripped over a downed tree before catching himself.

"Why'd you do that?"

"You're hiding them."

"What?"

"You put them back here in all this brush so none of your ritzy clients from the city would stumble across your dirty little secret. I dare you to deny it!"

"You don't know what you're talking about."

She folded her arms across her chest. "Are you telling me as big as this ranch is, this…" She gestured around them, her arms hitting branch after branch. "This is the best you can offer them?"

He moved closer to her. "They're satisfied with it, so what's it to you?"

"It's wrong!"

The pair stood in a stare off for several seconds before Dusty sighed. "Well, they're here now, so there is nothing I can do about it."

"Yes, there is! You can move them to a better location. Preferably *non-swamp* land." She lifted her feet to indicate the marshland beneath them.

A loud explosion sounded a few feet away, and Mikayla moved toward the sound. "What was that?"

"Probably Myron. He's the pyrotechnics guy."

"You have a pyrotechnics guy?" Her sunny disposition had returned and Dusty decided to get her through the brush before the righteous indignation returned.

"Yes, he's responsible for the fireworks and the cannon act."

They came out of the brush behind a row of large carts. A mischievous thought occurred to Dusty and before he could change his mind, he led Mikayla around the side of the third cart, making sure to keep her attention distracted by talking about the various acts of the show.

"But the real stars of the show are right here." He continued walking, then stopped in just the right spot. "Meet D'Angelo."

Mikayla looked over her shoulder and her eyes

widened to find herself looking into the golden-brown eyes of a tiger. His large body was less than two feet away, trapped behind closely spaced steel bars.

As awed as she was by his presence, D'Angelo looked far less impressed. Once he was satisfied they presented no danger and offered no food, he turned and sauntered back to the other side of the large cart where another smaller tiger lay dozing. "That's Marco."

"Wow," she whispered. "How old are they?"

Dusty tilted his head to the side. "Let me think. D'Angelo is the oldest—we've had him since I was about twelve. So I would say he's twenty-three. And Marco is a new addition. They picked him up after I'd left the show. Someone had him as a pet until he became too destructive, then they abandoned him to die. He was dehydrated and malnourished when the rescue group found him. They took him in to nurse him back to health, but really didn't have the facilities or funding to keep him. Normally, they don't give rescued animals to circuses, but my pop is friends with the guy who runs the program and, well...here's Marco."

Mikayla took a deep breath of air as if she were smelling a field of new flowers and not the various odors of animal life. She turned to Dusty with a smile. "I smell elephants?"

"I thought you'd never been to a circus?"

"I haven't, but I've been to a parade."

"Ahh." He took her hand once more and led her away from the big cats down a path lined with people doing various tasks.

Everyone they passed knew Dusty and stopped to wave or say hello. People dressed in various costumes, others dressed in jeans and T-shirts, some sorting through their equipment and others just idly watching life go by.

"Hey, Dusty, nice place!" someone called out.

Dusty threw up his hand at the guy Mikayla had not noticed. He appeared to be a trainer, given the way he led a horse in a tight circle.

"Who's that?" Mikayla asked.

Dusty's eyes narrowed on the guy's back. "Nobody."

He placed his hand around her waist and guided her away from the area, but Mikayla found herself looking back, wondering about the history between the two men.

Just then a three-foot clown jumped into their path and Mikayla caught herself just as she was about to shout, *"A midget!"*

She wasn't up on the politically correct term for little people, but she was fairly certain *that* was not it.

The clown blew his horn then stashed it in his pocket and pulled out a handkerchief. "He's going to do a trick!" Mikayla said with the excitement of a child.

Dusty smiled, realizing her enthusiasm was contagious. He started to introduce her to Herman, but decided that would spoil the moment. So he kept silent while the clown turned the one handkerchief into ten.

Mikayla clapped, and the clown bent at the waist in acceptance of the flattery. "You should keep this one, Dusty. I like her." Mikayla was taken aback at the deep baritone voice that came out of the little body.

"Of course you do, Herman. She's the only person

around here who hasn't seen you perform that trick eight hundred times."

Deciding to ignore Dusty altogether, Herman took Mikayla's hand and placed a small kiss on the back of it. "How do you do, my lady. Herman Mumfried at your service."

She smiled. "Nice to meet you, Herman. How very gallant you are."

Dusty just shook his head and the interplay and nudged Mikayla forward. "Okay, enough of this. Herman, do you know where my father is right now?"

"In his trailer, last I saw him."

"Thanks." Dusty guided Mikayla toward a grouping of mobile homes that formed what looked like a campsite unto themselves.

When they reached the trailer he was looking for, Dusty sighed in resignation. "You'd think after all these years, he would've bought a new one."

"Some things have sentimental value!" someone called from inside.

Dusty opened the door and poked his head in. "Pop? Are you decent, I have a lady with me."

"What would a lady be doing with you?" the voice asked.

"He's dressed," Dusty called back to Mikayla before opening the door to the trailer wider for her to enter.

As soon as she entered Mikayla was surprised by the comfy feel of the place. Pictures, pillows and plants spread all around; those things that can make any place feel like a home.

Kyle Warren got to his feet and Mikayla felt an instant

sense of déjà vu. There was no mistaking who Dusty took after.

He gave her a smile she knew so well. "Forgive me, I didn't think you were real. My son lies."

"No apology necessary." She leaned toward him. "I know what you mean."

Dusty frowned. "Hey—whose side are you on?"

"Yours, of course." She winked at Kyle.

"Okay." Dusty put up his hands in protest. "You two just met and you're already teaming up against me."

"Please, have a seat." Kyle brushed some papers off a nearby chair and gestured to Mikayla.

Dusty looked around for another empty chair, but saw none, except the one his father had just sat down in. "Where am I supposed to sit?"

Kyle shrugged. "Hell if I know. So, you must be Mikayla." Kyle said the name as if it had mystical powers. "What a beautiful name."

"Thank you," Mikayla said, trying to hide her amusement at Dusty's predicament as he emptied a milk crate, turned it upside down and made a makeshift chair.

"Dusty has told me all about you."

She glanced at Dusty over her shoulder. "Good stuff I hope."

"Nothing but." Kyle relaxed back in the chair. "So, what brings you waaaaay out here?"

Mikayla did not miss the emphasis. Apparently, Kyle realized his group had been hidden in the boondocks.

"Dusty just brought me down to look around after he found out I'd never been to a circus before."

Kyle looked as if the statement had been some kind of personal attack. "Never been to a circus? Ever?"

She shook her head.

"Well, that's outrageous! Your parents have a lot to answer for, young lady."

You have no idea, she thought, but held her tongue.

Kyle cast a knowing glance at Dusty before he leaned toward Mikayla. "You know, we could fix that in no time if Dusty here would just cooperate."

Dusty shot his father a warning glance. "Pop."

"What do you mean?" Mikayla asked, looking back and forth between the two men.

"Well—" Kyle's attempt at an innocent expression was anything but "—I was hoping we could put on some shows while we were here—after all, this is private property. Not a lot of shows, mind you, just a few. Just enough to earn the money for our license, but Dusty refuses."

Mikayla turned to Dusty. "Why won't you let them put on their show?"

Dusty glared at his father, but his words were directed at Mikayla. "I'll explain later."

"Sounds like a great idea," she continued. "I'm sure the people around here would love to see a circus act."

"Uh-huh." Dusty continued to glare at his father.

"And like he said, it would allow them the opportunity to make some income. What's not to like?"

"Uh-huh." Dusty turned to his father and whispered. "I'll get you back for this."

"It's not like you don't have the room or the resources," Mikayla went on, warming to the idea more and more. "They have everything they need. You're just providing land. What have you got to lose?"

Dusty stood. "Well, it's been nice visiting with you, Pop. I think we better be going now."

Kyle grinned. "The pleasure has been all mine." He took Mikayla's hand and stood with her. "And it was very nice meeting you, Mikayla. I hope to see you again soon."

She smiled at the older man. "If you do get to perform we definitely will—because I'll be in the front row."

As the couple made their way back to the house, Mikayla kept up her insistence that letting the circus perform was an excellent idea that served everyone involved. Dusty said nothing to dissuade her. He also said nothing to encourage her.

A short while later, he opened the back door of his house to let her go ahead of him, but she stopped and turned to him. "Well?"

"Well, what?"

"Are you going to let them perform?"

"Mikayla, it's not that simple. This is not just a ranch." He gestured over his shoulder. "I have a full-service hospital and stable. I have clients coming and going every day. If I give them free rein to this place—"

"Who said anything about free rein?" She moved closer to him and put her arms around his waist, bringing them face-to-face. "Look, I know you're uncomfortable with them here. I get it. But they can't leave until they get the money for the license, right?"

He begrudgingly agreed with a nod of his head.

"Okay, since you said Kyle won't simply take the money from you, give him a chance to make it on his own."

Dusty looked down into her eyes and knew for all

her logical arguments, she just wanted to see her first live circus. "Maybe. Let me think about it."

She smiled up a him. "Good enough."

She went into the house, and Dusty followed. He stopped in the doorway and glanced back toward the circus campsite. He'd known when he first received the letter that his father's presence on his ranch would complicate his life. He just hadn't expected it to happen this fast.

Ricardo Morgan, known as Rick to his friends, could not believe what he'd just seen. He spent the rest of the afternoon caring for his horses with a wide smile on his face. Despite his current troubles, she'd made his day. *Beautiful Tangie.*

Rick had believed she was dead. At least that was the story that circulated at the Godiva club, his favorite strip club whenever he was in Atlantic City. Word was one of the club patrons had attacked and killed her.

The club was well-known for its beautiful women, but Tangie was his main reason for returning to the club every time he stopped in the city. She was the stuff of wet dreams. And he'd masturbated many a night to the memory of her gyrating body as it stroked along the thin pole, imagining he was the pole. He even had a show bill with her on the cover. That was one fine woman, even after all these years, he thought. He shook his head to himself as he rubbed down one of his horses. It was good to know she was alive, even if she'd stopped dancing.

Once he saw the couple leave the camp, his curiosity overcame him and he went in search of Kyle. As he approached the trailer, he paused before knocking on the door.

He tried to think of a reason to give for coming to the trailer. After all, he knew Kyle would be suspicious if he just showed up asking questions about his son's girlfriend.

It wasn't always that way. Once the two men had been close as brothers, having come up in the business together. But while Kyle was putting his money away to start his own circus, Rick had been spending his on horse and dog races and looking for one big payoff.

Despite his bad habit, Kyle never said anything about it one way or the other. But all that changed about twenty years ago in Tulsa, when the two men went out drinking together and Rick's past caught up to both of them.

A local bookie he owed some money to wanted to send a message and he did. Three broken ribs, and a busted knee cap. Rick never walked the same again. The problem was the bookie in question was not very discriminating and Kyle had taken a fair share of the beating, as well, just for being in the wrong place at the wrong time.

It took several weeks for both of them to heal and after that things were never the same between them. But to Kyle's credit, a few years later when Rick had needed a job, Kyle had given him one and he'd been with the Warren circus ever since.

He remembered that he did have a legitimate reason to talk to Kyle about Dusty. He knocked on the door.

"Come in," Kyle called out.

Rick stuck his head around the door and smiled. "Got a minute?"

Kyle looked up from the book he was reading and Rick saw a wariness come into his eyes. "Sure, Rick. What can I do for you?"

Rick came into the trailer, closed the door behind him and leaned against it. "I just saw Dusty leaving."

Kyle smiled. "Yeah, I'm sorry our poor finances brought us here, but I am happy to spend some time with my son again."

Rick nodded in what he thought was a sympathetic manner. "Pretty girl with him."

Kyle's wary expression deepened. "Yes, she is."

Rick came farther into the trailer and leaned against the countertop. "Look, Kyle, I'm in a bit of trouble, and—"

Kyle held up his hands. "I'm broke, Rick—you know that."

"Not you," he said too quickly.

Kyle's eyes narrowed on him.

"I was just thinking, Dusty is doing so well, he wouldn't miss a few thousand."

"A few thousand!" He shook his head. "Damn, Rick, how much do you owe?"

"I'm not saying I want him to pay the whole amount." Rick tried to avoid answering the question. "I'm just saying anything he could spare. If you could talk to him—"

"Hell, no." Kyle turned his attention back to his book.

"He won't miss it. I mean, he's got money. A beautiful girl like Tan—like the one he was with doesn't come cheap."

"You leave Mikayla out of this!" Kyle pointed a finger at him.

Mikayla. Rick said the name again to himself, trying to memorize it.

"And she doesn't need Rick's money. She has enough of her own from her book sales."

Books. Rick bookmarked that bit of information, as well.

Kyle shook his head hard. "No, not this time, Rick. This time you are going to have to clean up your own mess."

Rick could see Kyle was getting upset, so he decided to back off for now. After all, they would be here for at least several weeks, plenty of time to approach him again. As for his fishing expedition, he had enough to start with. Her name was Mikayla, which was a somewhat uncommon name, and she wrote books.

He wondered if maybe all that was just a front for Dusty. If he was lucky, maybe she was still dancing at a club in the area. After all, stripper one day and author the next was unlikely. Still, as he left the trailer, he headed to his car. Time to find the local library and do a little research. He would find out one way or the other if Dusty's *Mikayla* was his *Tangie*.

Chapter 13

As Dusty approached the training building in his little golf cart, Sam came running toward him. "She's out again," he said, out of breath. Before Dusty could ask any questions, the other man shook his head. "Not sure when. Not sure how."

"Where is she now?" Dusty asked, looking in every direction for the reddish-gold dog that had become the bane of his existence.

"Not sure." Sam glanced at Dusty. "But I'm pretty certain I saw Athos and Porthos hanging around the fence earlier."

Dusty sighed. If they kept this up, he would have to start locking up his own dogs. "Okay, you check the stable. Given her penchant for trouble, I have an idea of where they might be headed."

He turned toward the new circus campsite. Taking Mikayla's advice, he'd moved the group to a better portion of land, closer to the stream. Although no one had openly complained about the previous location, they were all visibly happier to be in the new one.

As he drew closer, Dusty could see all types of commotion as the performers went about their routine. From the distance, nothing looked out of place.

He pulled to a stop at the end of the trailers and climbed out of the cart. He looked in the back and found a spare leash to take with him. He walked through the trailers, looking under each. He listened for the sound of dogs barking, but heard nothing.

As he came upon where the elephants were being hosed down, he stopped to question their trainer. "Hey, Troy, have you seen a group of unfamiliar dogs come through here?"

Troy nodded. "Matter of fact, I did. I just assumed Walt had found a couple of new dogs for his show." He gestured over his left shoulder. "They went that way."

"Thanks." Dusty followed the path and ended up right back where he started at the trailers, but this time he was at the opposite end. As he approached his father's trailer, he heard Kyle's voice coming from around the corner.

When he rounded the corner he was stunned to see Kyle standing before a row of four obedient dogs sitting on their haunches. Apparently, Sam had missed little Aramis.

The dogs watched the actions of Kyle's hands so intently, they never noticed Dusty. Kyle was watching them just as intently as he gave a command in a stern voice. "Up!" He gestured again and Dusty watched in amazement as all four dogs stood to their feet.

Kyle crossed and tucked a dog treat in each of the mouths. The dogs gobbled it and stood, tails wagging, waiting for more.

Dusty came forward, clapping his hands. "Bravo! I had forgotten what a great animal trainer you are."

Kyle was not appeased by the compliment. He turned to his son. "Dusty, what the hell are you doing letting these dogs run wild? We could've had a mess this morning when they came running through the camp. They got D'Angelo in an uproar. It took Arturo twenty minutes to settle him down again."

"Sorry," he said, feeling like a disobedient child. "This is Angel, Mikayla's dog. I'm training her."

Kyle laughed. "Training her to what? Get someone killed?"

Dusty, feeling more than a little defensive, crossed and placed the leash on Angel's collar before she realized what was happening. "Calm down. She's not dangerous. Just high-strung."

"That high-strung nature almost made her tiger bait this morning," Kyle continued to rant. "These animals may be tamed, but they are still animals with free will and unpredictable natures."

Dusty realized this was a losing argument either way so he said nothing.

"That's Mikayla's dog?" Kyle asked with a strange expression.

"Yes." Dusty guided Angel away from his father and the other dogs, but she tugged at the leash until Dusty dropped it. Then she sauntered back over to Kyle.

"Humph." Kyle shrugged. "You'd think a pretty little thing like her would have one of those little purse dogs, not this old girl." He patted Angel's head and she lifted her ears clearly enjoying it.

Dusty gave Angel a questioning look. "Yeah, well, Mikayla loves the mutt so I am determined to train her."

"Son, son, son." Kyle shook his head. "I thought I taught you better than that."

Dusty just looked at his father in confusion.

"Don't you think she senses your aggression?" He chuckled. "Hell, I can feel it from over here."

"What do you mean?"

"Animals are intuitive. They have to be. And she knows you don't like her. Of course she is going to resist."

Dusty's confused expression turned wary. "Um, Pop...she's a dog."

"Exactly why you should be a little smarter in how you deal with her. She only sees you when you are in trainer mode." Kyle patted his leg and the dogs trotted over to him.

Kyle knelt among the dogs, patting their heads and rubbing under their chins. "You have to be more than just a disciplinarian. Spend some time with her, let her know you are her friend."

Dusty looked at the dog who was staring up at his father in the same adoring manner in which she watched Mikayla. Maybe Kyle was onto something, Dusty thought. Maybe Angel did sense his frustration and anger when he dealt with her.

Later, instead of taking Angel back to the training facility, he took her home with him, along with Athos,

Porthos and Aramis. He needed to find a way to bond with her.

In the morning, he and Mikayla were flying up to Tallahassee for one of her seminars, so he knew she would be arriving early. If he could make some strides toward improving things with Angel before then, he thought, it would look good.

He spent the evening playing with the dogs in the yard and had to admit when she was not being a stubborn mule, Angel was really adorable. She was very smart and playful, and he was beginning to understand Mikayla's affection for her.

That night, after he'd fed them he considered locking Angel up, but decided not to. He never locked his three dogs up and he was trying to win her trust. When he climbed the stairs to his bedroom, all the dogs, including Angel, were lying on the deck, enjoying the evening breeze.

The next morning, Dusty heard his doorbell ringing, and realized he'd overslept. He wondered why the alarm clock had not gone off as he stumbled half-asleep to the front door. He opened it to find a bright, fresh Mikayla holding a tray of coffee and a bag of bagels.

"Morning!" She placed a quick kiss on his lips before moving past him into the house. "I thought you might be a little out of it, getting up so early, so I brought breakfast."

Dusty closed the door and started to follow her into the kitchen, but she had stopped just outside the living room doors. Her whole body went rigid and when Dusty came up beside her he could see why.

He was instantly awake as his eyes widened in horror. "What the hell!"

He walked into what looked like a war zone. His brown leather couch had been ripped to shreds, the puffy white stuffing was scattered throughout the room. His throw pillows had met the same fate. His favorite crystal vase lay in fragments on the tufted carpet that had also been shredded. The coffee table was tipped over and the ceramic centerpiece that sat on it had been shattered.

Dusty was shell-shocked. Everywhere he looked there were pieces of his possessions, and lying smack dab in the center of the ruined couch sat Angel. Her tongue lolling to the side, her eyes shining and not a inch of remorse in her whole body. Her tail wagged to see Mikayla, and what really pissed Dusty off was the damn dog looked as if she were smiling. *Smiling!*

On the other side of the room, his three dogs were all cowering under the only piece of standing furniture—a marble-top side table. They watched him with anxious eyes, but Dusty knew they were not responsible for this mess. His narrowed gaze returned to Angel. He knew who had done this, and he was going to kill her.

As if reading his thoughts, Mikayla stepped in front of him to block his view of the dog. "Now, Dusty, I know you're angry, but she's just a dog. I'll pay for any damages, just give me an estimate of the cost—"

"Hannah was right—she *is* a hellhound."

"Dusty…" Mikayla watched him closely. "What are you thinking?"

He looked at Mikayla with a strange smile. "Don't

worry, sweetheart. When you euthanize a dog they don't even feel it."

Her eyes widened. "Euthanize!" She shook her head. "I don't think so!"

His eyes narrowed on her face. "It's either that or I kill her with my bare hands!"

"Sorry—neither of those are acceptable options." She glanced around the room as if unable to look at it for long. "What was she doing here, anyway? I thought you locked her up at night."

He nodded. "Normally we do, at the training facility, but I wanted some time to try to…to…" He sighed as if even confessing it hurt. "I was trying to bond with her." He looked at Mikayla. "But you can't bond with the devil."

"She's no devil." Mikayla crossed the room to Angel. "She's just high-strung."

"Oh, give it up!" he snapped. "That's the same lie I tried to tell my fath—" His expression took on a new look, one of dawning comprehension. "This is his fault," he whispered.

"What? Whose fault?" Mikayla asked, sitting down beside Angel and putting her arm around the dog.

"My father. He's the one who told me to *be her friend*. Ha! See how well that worked out!" He noticed how quiet Mikayla was, and when he looked at her she was watching him with a warm expression.

He frowned. "What?"

"You were trying to bond with her…for me, weren't you?"

The gentle question in her eyes seemed to calm his temper a bit. "I haven't been honest with you about her training so far. I've kinda led you to believe I'm making more progress than I am. Truth is, she's fought me every step of the way, and as you can see..." He gestured to the sofa. "She's no more disciplined today than she was four weeks ago."

"Why didn't you say anything?"

Instead of answering, he started collecting the pieces of the crystal vase from the floor, but he could feel Mikayla's eyes on him.

"Dusty, I love Angel, I do. But our relationship has nothing to do with whether or not you can train my dog."

He stood and turned to her. "And what if it becomes more?"

"What *if* it becomes more? What do you mean?"

"What if this relationship develops into something more serious? Something...long lasting?"

Mikayla looked away. "We'll deal with it when the time comes."

Just then, a knock on the back door came before it was opened. Dusty never locked it and most of the staff knew that.

"Hello?" Sam called from the kitchen.

"In here, Sam," Dusty called back.

As he came into the living room, Sam stopped suddenly just as they had earlier. "Damn! What happened in here?"

"Angel happened," Dusty said.

Sam glanced at Dusty's tense stance, and then over at the couch where Mikayla was huddled over Angel. "I guess it's good I showed up when I did, huh?"

He patted his leg and called to Angel and she hopped

off the couch and rushed to him like she was greeting an old friend. The other dogs followed, as well.

"Mind if I take her for her workout?" Sam asked.

Dusty gestured for him to take her.

After Sam and the dogs disappeared out the back, Dusty and Mikayla were left alone in the quiet house. After a while, Dusty looked at Mikayla. "You won't give me anything, will you?"

Mikayla looked up with a confused expression. "Excuse me?"

"You won't tell me anything about yourself, and you won't even give me the comfort of believing we have something real here."

"That's not true. I've told you how I feel about you. I just don't want to get ahead of ourselves."

He stared at her for several seconds before shaking his head. "Whatever." He tossed the shards of crystal on the side table. "I'm going to get a shower." He turned and headed to the stairs.

Chapter 14

The one-and-a-half-hour flight to Tallahassee was tension personified. The pair barely spoke to one another, only exchanging words when absolutely necessary.

It wasn't until they were in the rental car that Mikayla spoke directly to him. "You know, you didn't have to come up here with me today."

"Don't be ridiculous—I wanted to."

After that exchange they drove in silence a while longer with Mikayla behind the wheel. "Just so you know, my seminars cater to women, so it may not be anything you would find useful."

"I'm okay with it."

They pulled into the hotel where the seminar was being held. She parked the car and turned in the seat to face him. "If you want to take the car and do a little sightseeing instead, I wouldn't be offended."

Looking into her eyes, Dusty realized the anxiety he

was feeling coming off of her had nothing to do with what had happened that morning. For whatever reason, she was nervous about the seminar.

"Mikayla, if you did not want me here, why did you invite me?"

"I want you here," she said. "Really, I do. I just don't want you to feel obligated to stay if you don't want to."

She was conflicted, he thought. "No, I want to stay. Who knows, maybe I'll learn something today."

She forced a smile. "Okay, it's your decision."

Dusty had known Mikayla was a popular speaker, but it wasn't until he saw her in this setting that he fully understood the extent of her popularity. The moment she walked through the door the women gathered around her as if they'd known each other for years, and spoke to her with a familiarity that Dusty found fascinating. And the most interesting factor of all was that Mikayla seemed to relish it. It was a different side of her, one he'd never imagined existed. Before his eyes she'd transformed from the somber, reserved woman he knew into an outgoing bubble of charisma and energy.

But once they were backstage and away from the crowd she reverted back to the Mikayla he was most familiar with. The one he felt he had to pry open with a crowbar.

An hour later, he left her backstage, waiting to be introduced, and took a seat in the back of a crowded banquet hall of about three hundred women and very few men.

The mistress of ceremonies came onto the stage and for the next several minutes, listed all of Mikayla's accomplishments over the past five years, but Dusty's attention was drawn to the fact that nothing was said about her childhood or her early life experiences. It was as if she'd been born with the release of her book.

He felt a sinking feeling in the pit of his stomach, as he was forced to admit something he'd fought hard not to. Mikayla Shroeder was hiding something.

Up until now, he'd wanted to believe her refusal to share anything about her past had something to do with her fear of commitment. If that had been the case, he was sure he could overcome it. But whatever she was hiding, she was hiding not only from him, but from the world.

He watched her take the stage with exuberance, and the crowd totally responded to her. It didn't take him long to understand that for Mikayla this wasn't about selling her books, it was about the women in the audience. He looked over the crowd and saw them for the first time. Really saw them. Only then did he notice the telltale signs.

Many of them bore the evidence of years of abuse in the form of healed scars, and sadly, some of the scars were fresh. He noticed one woman clutching Mikayla's book to her chest as if it held all the secrets of life, and he realized that for her it did.

To her, to most of these women, Mikayla was more than a motivational speaker, she was a sister spirit. She was a Valkyrie. A warrior who'd walked through the fire and come out on the other side. Like Dusty, they understood in some collective way that there were secrets in her past she was not willing to share. At least not yet. But together they silently acknowledged what he was now coming to understand.

Whatever Mikayla had been through had made her a stronger woman and now she was trying to pass that strength on to them. And whether she was conscious of it or not, Mikayla needed them as much as they needed her.

Watching her move across the stage, telling funny stories, many of which included Angel, he couldn't help but feel a sense of pride in her. There was so much more to her, and he was hoping he would have a lifetime to learn every single thing about her.

Mikayla had to be the most complicated and the most difficult woman he'd ever met. And in that moment he realized he loved her, from the way she opened her soul to him when they made love to the way she closed herself up in a brick fortress afterward. Dusty decided right then it would be his life mission to knock down the walls, stone by stone, brick by brick, painful memory by painful memory. He made a promise to himself, one day he would own her heart as she owned his.

As she spoke to the young woman she'd brought to the stage, a girl named Marie, Mikayla fought back the tears. Marie couldn't have been more than nineteen, and she reminded Mikayla so much of herself after the attack.

She could see the resolve in Marie's eyes. A change was in the making. This young woman was evolving, and Mikayla knew from firsthand experience that process was different for everyone.

Marie had taken the microphone and was telling the

crowd about the first time she read one of the exercises in Mikayla's book. It gave steps to evaluating your life. She was telling the crowd how for the first time she began to realize she was in a downward spiral of self-destruction, and during the telling of her story, when the memories became too much, Marie gave in to the tears. Which caused Mikayla to give in to her tears. Faces throughout the crowd were reflections of Marie, and Mikayla found herself drawing on pools of strength she did not know she had, hoping in some small way she could transfer it to the crowd gathered here.

Her eyes scanned the group and she found Dusty at the back of the room. He sat at a table, watching her with those compassionate eyes that first made her love him.

Her heart was torn in two over the man. For too many years she taught herself not to trust, and the lesson had been effective. Too effective.

Because now, when she wanted to trust, when she had a reason to trust she couldn't seem to bring herself to do it. Mikayla had done the only thing she could think to do. She'd brought him into her world. She'd asked him to come with her today because she wanted him to see, to witness, to share, to know.

It was as if she were screaming from her soul, *Stop searching for what I used to be—just love what I've become.*

And he did. She could see it in his eyes. He understood, at least as much as he could. Over the past few weeks, she'd fought so hard to open the door of her heart, but fear, an overwhelming fear would stop her in her tracks every time.

In truth, she did not even understand it. It wasn't like she was recovering from a broken heart. What had happened to her had nothing to do with love, and yet her ability to love seemed to have been a casualty of the attack.

She had not realized it until now because she hadn't met anyone like Dusty before. And she was terrified she was going to lose him if she did not find some way to connect to him. Some way to show him how much she loved him. How much she needed him. She tried with her body, she tried to give him everything when they made love. But she knew he needed more. And she had no idea if she was even capable of giving him more.

Marie finished her story, and Mikayla hugged her close, trying to infuse her with courage to take back to the battlefield that was her life.

Mikayla forced her attention away from Dusty and back to the crowd of women who'd come to see her, many of whom had traveled far to be there. Over the next two hours, they laughed together, they cried together, and she spoke of method after method of how they, too, could turn their lives around. Methods that had taken her years to perfect. She was proud of her book and the lives she'd changed.

That evening as they were driving back to the airport, Dusty tried to avoid discussing what he'd seen that morning. He knew Mikayla had had enough of an emotional rollercoaster ride for one day.

"I've made a decision," he announced.

She glanced at him with a wary expression. "Oh? What would that be?"

"I've decided not to euthanize Angel."

She arched an eyebrow. "Glad to hear it. Because if you had so much as hurt a hair on her head, I would have to hurt you."

"How would you know?"

"How would I know what?"

"If I'd hurt a hair on her head. Her fur is so matted you wouldn't be able to tell."

She frowned. "Look, she can't help it if she has funky hair."

"You know I'm a trained professional and even I can't tell with certainty what breeds she comes from."

"It doesn't matter. She's my baby, and you're not allowed to kill her, no matter how much she may deserve it."

"You owe me a couch—and a vase. Oh, and some more throw pillows."

"I know." She sighed. "You were our last hope for any training. I'd heard you were pretty good."

"I'm damn good!" he said in an offended tone. "With dogs."

"What are you saying, she's not a dog?" Mikayla laughed, and it was music to Dusty's ears. He'd hope to lighten the mood, and it seemed to be working.

"I'm just saying until I can identify her origins... Remember the story years ago about that couple that brought home what they thought was a Chihuahua from Mexico and it turned out to be a rat?"

She burst into laughter. "That's just an urban legend!"

He shrugged. "Stranger things have happened."

"Believe me, she's a dog. Just your standard, run-of-the-mill mutt."

"So you say."

"Since you've failed so miserably, can I take her home now?"

He shook his head. "Nope. I said eight weeks, and it's only been four. Who knows, maybe I'll manage a miracle in the next four."

"Or maybe she'll crush your spirit completely, and you'll retire a broken man having met his match."

"We'll see."

"I told you she was stubborn."

"And I told you, so am I."

"Well." She leaned over and kissed his cheek. "May the best mammal win."

Chapter 15

Rick saw them before they saw him—Leo's goons, three of them, large and muscular and looking more than capable of breaking a man in half. He cut through the crowded clubhouse in hopes of making it to the exit before he was spotted. He kept his head down and slumped his shoulders, but he forgot about the all-seeing eyes in the ceiling.

As he approached the exit, he spotted two goons ahead of him. They were watching the crowd and Rick knew right away they were looking for him. He turned and started toward the back entrance leading to the stables, but by then the other goons had caught up to him.

Two of the burly men grabbed his arms and led him toward the exit. "Leo's been looking for you, Rick."

Rick forced a laugh. "Why would Leo be looking for me?"

"I think you know why," the man to the right said, and squeezed his arm a little tighter.

Rick swallowed hard and looked around, hoping for a miracle, wondering if he'd seen his last day.

Outside the stable sat a row of cars. The two men led him to a burgundy-colored Chrysler Three Hundred and forced him inside, each climbing in on either side of him. A third man was in the driver's seat and he started the car.

As they drove, Rick's mind was racing, trying to find a way to save his life. He considered anything he owned that could be sold, but one of the disadvantages of being a carnie was that you tended to collect only the things that traveled light, and that did not include a lot of material wealth.

His eyes narrowed as he replayed the conversation he'd had with Kyle the night before. It was the same one he'd been having with the old man almost every day since they'd arrived at the ranch. But the asshole refused to ask Dusty for any money even if it meant his life.

Rick knew Dusty would never give the money to him because he would assume it was to pay gambling debts. And *Mr. Self-Righteous* was too high and mighty for that. No, they had too much history and Dusty never liked him anyway, even when he was a kid. At least Kyle didn't judge him, he just refused to help him.

Maybe if he broke into the house and stole some stuff; Dusty probably had all kinds of big-screen televisions, and computer equipment. Maybe he could sneak into the animal hospital one night—there was all kinds of stuff in there, including drugs.

Rick glanced at the two men sandwiching him in and mentally compared them to Dusty. Neither was a good choice. With these men, he could assume they had the kinds of skills that made them very good in their line of work, but with Dusty…he knew what he was capable of. He'd once seen the youngster almost kill a man over a damn car.

No, dealing with Dusty's wrath if he was discovered breaking into his house or hospital was in no way a better option than whatever Leo had planned for him.

They drove into a part of Miami Rick had never seen before and pulled up in front of a dive. Rick was more than a little taken aback. The last time he'd seen Leo, which was three years ago, the loan shark had been doing much better than this.

"Leo is *here?*"

The goon to his right nodded. "Let's go." He opened the door and taking Rick by the arm, pulled him out of the car.

Rick was beginning to feel a little better. If Leo had sunk to this maybe he wouldn't be so hard to please. Maybe he could get by paying off half his loan amount. A desperate man will deal.

They led him down a long, dim hallway to a door at the back. The goon sitting on his left during the car ride made a weird sort of rapping noise on the door, and someone inside said come in.

As soon as the door opened and Rick saw the scene inside, the good feeling drained out of his body. Before him stood Leo, looking every bit the successful business-man he remembered. He was staring down at a sheet of plastic on the floor. On the plastic was a heap of something that used to be human, covered in blood and barely breathing.

The man had been so badly beaten his face was unrecognizable. The goon obviously responsible for the assault—since Leo didn't have so much as a speck of blood on his shoe—was wiping his bloody hands on a large white towel that was quickly becoming reddish-brown.

One of the two goons with him pushed Rick into the room, and that caught Leo's attention. He looked at Rick and smiled. He actually smiled!

Rick stared back in terror.

"Ricardo! Long time, no see, huh?" He held out his arms. "Come give your Uncle Leo a hug."

Rick could not have moved his feet if he wanted to.

Leo's smile faded. "I said come give your Uncle Leo a hug."

Finding courage he did not know he possessed, Rick moved across the room, but stopped at the edge of the plastic.

"Just go around." Leo gestured to the plastic and Rick did.

Soon he was enclosed in a bear hug that felt like genuine fondness, but he knew better than to let himself believe it.

"I heard around that you and all your circus freak buddies were back in town, so imagine my surprise when I don't get so much as a phone call, saying, 'Hey Leo, I'm back in town.'"

"I was going to call you, Leo," Rick lied, hoping it sounded like truth.

"Sure you were. Sure you were. But you took so long

I decided to look you up instead." He wrapped his beefy arm around Rick's shoulder and guided him to a nearby table. "Have a seat." He gestured to a chair and Rick sat.

"So, how you been? How's business?" Leo asked.

"Okay, I guess. Look, Leo, I haven't forgot you. I'm going to get your money."

Leo's eyes widened in surprise. "Have I said anything about the fifty grand you owe me?" He looked at his three employees. "You hear me say anything about money?" They all shook their heads in response, before Leo turned back. "Here I am trying to have a nice little reunion with an old friend and you go bringing up some…unpleasantness."

"I just wanted you to know I wasn't trying to skip out on you."

Leo's smile disappeared. "No, you already did that—three years ago."

Rick swallowed hard, seeing the raw rage in the man. Everything before had been just a show. This was the true Leo, the man who ruled Miami's underworld with an iron fist. This was the man who haunted his dreams.

Leo cleared his throat. "I was hoping we could have some refreshments, and maybe a little time to catch up, but okay. You want to get straight to business." He sat back and laced his fingers over his large belly, and Rick tried to ignore the three goons as they wrapped up the plastic and carried it out of the room.

Leo's brown eyes narrowed to slits. "Where the hell is my money, Rick?"

"I'm getting it, Leo. I swear I am."

"You've been getting it for three years."

"I know. I know. But I ran into some hard times."

"You think I want to hear any bullshit about your hard times? You're still breathing, aren't you? Couldn't have been that tough."

"Leo, please, just give me a little longer."

Leo simply stared at him for a long time before he nodded. "I like you, Rick. Always have. You remind me of my sister's kid. He's a worthless sack of shit, too, but he has a good heart. In fact, liking you is why I brought you here." He gestured around the room.

"This is where I deal with those who don't pay me back." He gestured to the door. "Like Mikey, there. I gave him every opportunity to pay me my money and he thought I was playing some kind of game or something, because he never took me seriously. I ask nicely, and if that don't work I bring you here and ask not so nicely. This place is like hell, Rick. Once you enter you never leave. You getting me?"

Rick nodded.

Leo licked his lips and Rick couldn't help thinking of a tiger that had just finished its meal. "But today, I'm going to make an exception. Today, for you, this place is purgatory."

Rick frowned in confusion.

"I'm going to let you go today, but what you do after you leave this room will determine whether you end up in heaven or hell." Leo dropped his hands from his stomach and stood. "Get my money by the end of the week, Rick. Or the next time you see this room, you won't be leaving."

Rick stood on shaking legs, not actually believing he

was being let go. He inched toward the door and when Leo made no move to stop him he bolted the last few steps.

He yanked open the door and Leo's words stopped him. "The end of the week, Rick." Leo turned to look at him. "And keep in mind, me liking you won't save you again."

It took Rick a couple of hours to find his way back to a part of town he recognized and even then he was still edgy looking over his shoulders. He couldn't believe it. Leo was not exactly known for his benevolent nature, so Rick kept thinking it was all some kind of cruel trick. He found his car just where he'd left it at the dog track and hurried back to the camp, back to the ranch where it was safe.

From the time he joined his first circus twenty-three years ago, the circus had felt like home. Working with the horses was as soothing a life as any man could ask for…but the itch. The uncontrollable itch to test his skills against lady luck. That itch had been his downfall as far back as he could remember. That itch was about to get him killed.

As he pulled through the gates to the Warren ranch, he had mixed feelings.

One, the sense of safety he felt in the presence of other carnies, and a sense of resentment that Dusty had acquired so much in his short life and wasn't willing to share it with them, his family. He was hoarding it all to himself.

It wasn't right.

As he entered his trailer a short while later, the fear was beginning to subside. He stretched out across his bed and focused his mind. He had to get Leo his money by the end of the week. He had no intention of ever seeing that room again, except in his nightmares.

He thought about asking Kyle to go to Dusty on his behalf once more, but he knew when Kyle made up his mind about something that was that. And going to Dusty directly was out of the question. He racked his brain, thinking of anyone else he knew that had that kind of money. Suddenly, it hit him.

He hopped off the bed and reached beneath the mattress for his magazines. He flipped through the magazines until he found what he was looking for. The show bill he'd saved from the night the club finally featured her. He'd been waiting months for a show bill with her on the front of it. And there she was. The beautiful, incomparable Tangie. Or as she was now known, Mikayla Shroeder. She had money, plenty of money. And he was willing to bet she'd pay a nice bit of it to keep her little secret a secret.

Rick smiled to himself. Lady luck had decided he deserved a break. Maybe this was the beginning of a winning streak. He considered driving back into the city, but with Leo's goons all over the place he decided that wasn't the best idea.

He tucked his magazines back in place and headed out of the trailer, looking for a few guys to sucker into a few hands of poker.

Chapter 16

Mikayla sat beside Dusty on the hard bench and held her breath as Joannie maneuvered across the tightrope thirty feet over their heads.

She leaned toward Dusty and whispered. "This is nerve-racking!"

Dusty smiled. "Just remember, Chris has been doing this for fifteen years, and Joannie has been doing it for eight. They know what they're doing."

Still the drumroll played in the background, the bright spotlight shone on the young girl, who looked so tiny far overhead, and Mikayla found herself clutching Dusty's hands in her own.

After what seemed an eternity to the people below, Joannie reached the other side, turned and took a small bow to the loud applause of the crowd. Without hesitation, she then reached up and grabbed the swinging bar and swung out over the crowd to meet her partner Chris on the other side.

"Know how they met?" Dusty whispered.

"How?"

"They were competing for the same job with a circus in Russia and while they were waiting to audition, they got the idea if they presented themselves as a team they would have a better chance."

"But they didn't even know each other. How could they audition together?"

He looked down into her eyes. "Sometimes, the rhythm is just right. Some people have that kind of chemistry."

She smiled. "Oh, really?"

"Yep."

"You know anyone else with that kind of chemistry?"

His smiled turned into a grin. "As a matter of fact, I do." He placed a quick kiss on the tip of her nose and turned his attention back to the show.

When Mikayla looked around Joannie and Chris were gone and the equestrian portion of the show was beginning. She wondered how had he distracted her so she hadn't even noticed the change.

They watched the entire show, eating everything that passed on the aisle way from cotton candy to hot dogs. Halfway through the show, Mikayla looked up at Dusty to find him watching the show with an almost dreamy expression.

"What are you thinking?"

He looked at her with the same expression. "I had forgotten how much I loved this."

She frowned. "Then why did you leave it?"

"No, you misunderstand. I love the circus. I do not love circus life." He shook his head. "Living in twelve different cities in a week. Do you have any idea how many schools I've attended in my lifetime?" He held up his fingers as if counting and then sighed in frustration. "Damn, I forgot. I used to know."

Mikayla reached up and touched his face. "It's okay. I understand—I do. You wanted some sense of stability. I can relate."

"Can you?" he asked, his eyes watching her face. "Where did you grow up?" Dusty saw the veil of distrust come over her eyes.

"Up north," she said, and then began clapping as the riders all stood on the backs of the horses in unison.

Dusty knew he would get nothing else out of her about where she grew up. It was amazing the way they spent so much time together, so much time just talking, and yet he still knew so little about her.

He studied her pretty profile, wondering if he would ever be allowed to know the whole woman. She started laughing and he realized it was because the clowns had come in. Eight little people all dressed in suspenders and firemen hats climbed out of a tiny car. It was one of the oldest plays in the book and yet it never failed to make the crowd laugh. Dusty had often thought it was like watching a favorite episode of a television show again and again. Even though you already knew everything that was going to happen, you still loved it.

A few minutes later, the clowns climbed back into their car and rolled away and in rolled a giant cannon.

"Ah, here's me."

"What?"

He gestured to the cannon. "From age twelve to sixteen I was the human cannon."

Mikayla's eyes widened. "Isn't that a bit young to be shooting you out of a cannon?"

He laughed. "Sweetheart, they weren't *actually* shooting me out of the cannon."

She frowned in disappointment. "They don't?"

Dusty paused, wondering if he should say any more. The look on her face looked as if he had just told her there was no Santa Claus.

"You have to remember in the circus, a kid is put to work as soon as he can walk. You are taught the life from day one."

She smiled. "Well, I'm just glad it didn't do any permanent damage."

They watched as a boy of about fourteen waved to the crowd before climbing into the cannon.

"That's Curran, Alexia's son."

"Alexia the fire eater?" she asked with awe.

"The one and only. You didn't get a chance to meet her the other day, did you?"

She shook her head. "Okay, I'll introduce you later."

She beamed up at him as if he'd just offered to introduce her to her favorite rock star. If he'd known she loved the circus so much, Dusty thought, he would've invited his family to come stay awhile ago.

They watched the show until the very last elephant had taken its victory lap around the tent and the crowds were clearing out.

From where he sat Dusty could see most of the people

were locals, but many he'd never seen before. Which just went to show, when the circus was in town people would find it.

Afterward, as promised, Dusty led Mikayla back to Alexia's trailer to introduce her. When Mikayla produced a copy of the program and asked Alexia to sign, Dusty almost laughed out loud, but wisely held it in as Alexia autographed the program.

After he checked in with his father to be sure everything was under control, he led her back up to the house, taking the long route along the stream that ran through the property.

Walking hand in hand over the lush grass, Mikayla asked, "Why did you buy so much property? I mean, you use about a quarter of it for your house and the hospital."

"Overcompensating, I guess."

She laughed. "You have nothing to compensate for."

"Thanks." He flashed her a brief grin.

"Seriously, why so much? Granted it comes in handy when your family arrives, but I don't think you bought it with them in mind."

He thought about the question for a while before answering. He could give her some witty little response, but he wanted her to know the truth. He wanted her to know him, and he hoped it would allow her to open up so he could get to know her.

"Think of it like a kid who grows up with too little to eat. They are the people who become hoarders later in life. Or the runt who's always trying to prove himself.

"In a way it really is overcompensating. I never had

anything of my own, no home except the circus. I never lived in a house or even an apartment. So as soon as I could afford to I bought up as much land as I could. Something completely mine." He touched an oak tree as they passed by it, running his hand over the rough bark. "Mine." He whispered the word, but in the silence of the night, Mikayla heard.

He stopped and turned her to face him, then looking deep into her eyes, he repeated the one word, "Mine," and lowered his lips to hers.

Mikayla opened to him. Wrapping her arms around his neck she pulled him closer until she could feel his body against her own.

His hands roamed over her blue-jeans-clad body touching every curve, every line. He'd memorized every inch of her and his fingers remembered. Soon his warm mouth was on her neck as his tongue traced every vein, sending chill after chill through her whole being.

Mikayla could feel his growing erection against her stomach and she wanted nothing more than to lie down on the damp grass with him.

But instead, he took her hand and started running. "Come on."

"Where are we going?"

"To the house, to my bed."

She followed him as he led her through the trees with the sure step of someone who'd traveled that way many times before. He was right, this was his land, his home, and he cared for every bit of it. The parts seen and appreciated by people and the parts never to be known to anyone but him.

Mikayla knew that was how Dusty would love a

woman. Every part of her. The surface beauty the world saw, and the soul of a woman. Dusty would want to know the soul of his woman and Mikayla was not sure she was ready to share her soul with him or anyone else, for that matter.

As those thoughts raced through her mind, they came upon the back entrance into his elegant brick house. And within minutes they were both inside. Dusty never slowed.

Mikayla noticed the quiet right away. "Where are the dogs?"

"They come and go as they please, through the door in the kitchen." He continued to pull her along through the house and up the stairs, stopping when they reached his bedroom. "With everything going on down at the circus camp, I'm sure they're getting into trouble."

He shut the door behind them and turned to face her. "Finally."

She smiled. "In a hurry, are we?"

He laughed. "Yes, but that's not what I meant." He wrapped his arms around her waist. "Since the first time we made love, I've wanted you back here in my bed, here with me."

She glanced back over her shoulder at the big bed. She'd been here before with him many times, but he was right. Up until tonight they'd only made love there once.

"Does your bed have some kind of magical powers that makes sex better?"

He kissed her neck, picking up right where he'd left off. "No, but I want to wake up every morning and remember you lying next to me. I want to walk through that door at night and see your beautiful, naked body waiting for me. And I have a good imagination and all, but there is nothing like the real thing."

"Well, here I am." She lifted both arms and Dusty took the opportunity to lift her cotton top over her head along with her bra, and in one fluent motion she was topless.

"Now, just do that with your legs and we'll be good to go." He grinned.

She turned, casting a seductive look over her shoulder and walked to the bed. "No, you've got to work a little harder to get in my pants."

"Since when?"

She turned with a frown. "What's that supposed to mean?"

He caught up with her and began planting kisses on her face, neck and shoulders even as his hands covered her bare breasts. "Nothing, nothing. I meant nothing. Don't get mad—not now," he whispered.

And the kisses seemed to appease her because he could feel her relaxing in his arms. She began unbuttoning his plaid shirt. He was eager to help her, giving up on the buttons and pulling it over his head.

The motion carried them both over and onto the bed where they never let go of one another. Soon they were a tangle of blue-jeans-clad legs and bare breasts to bare chest, letting their mouths guide the way as they licked and sucked and tongued every inch of bare skin available.

Mikayla felt as if the hot, throbbing penis pressing against the blue jean material was going to pop the bottoms, but still Dusty held her with gentle arms and kissed her with the slow caress of a man who had nothing but time. His large hands roamed over every inch of her, touching, squeezing and claiming until her whole body was arching in need.

He climbed off the bed and removed his own jeans and underwear before pulling hers off. She waited with what little patience she could form as he dug around in his nightstand and found a condom. He donned it and then he was back over her flesh to flesh, ache for ache, and Mikayla wasn't sure how much longer she could wait.

With precision, he pressed his penis against her wet opening, careful not to enter her just yet. He was torturing her, and Mikayla moved her body in every imaginable way, trying to force him to give her what she needed.

But he knew what she was doing, and held himself away.

"Please," she whimpered, needing him to finish, to complete her, to make the aching stop.

"No, baby, I can't." He kissed her shoulder.

"It's okay," she whispered, running her fingers across the hard planes of his back. The moisture in the middle told her he was as desperate for her as she was for him. "It's okay."

He pressed his face against her neck and she felt his whole body shake with a suppressed shudder. As if surrendering to something stronger than himself, he shifted his body, lifted her hips and plunged deep inside of her.

Mikayla could not hold back the cry of pleasure that exploded through her whole being. It was as if he'd set off some kind of incendiary device in the center of her body and she felt herself convulsing as wave after wave of indescribable pleasure flowed through her.

Dusty released his own cry of pleasure, as he shifted his body once more, putting his weight on his hands as he plowed into her body. All Mikayla could do was hold on to his muscular arms as he poured himself inside her.

Several minutes later, the pair lay cuddled together. Mikayla's head rested on Dusty's chest. Dusty lay with his one arm wrapped around Mikayla and the other folded behind his head.

"Mikayla?"

"Hmm." She yawned. The aftereffects of lovemaking with Dusty were always the same; complete and utter exhaustion.

"What city did you grow up in?"

She was quiet so long, he wondered if she had indeed fallen off to sleep.

"Why?"

"Because you have never told me. You say things like, 'up north' or 'an urban area.' I'm not even sure what the hell that means."

"What does it matter?"

"It's a part of you."

She was quiet again for a long time before she said, "Atlantic City."

Dusty smiled, feeling as if he'd won some kind of contest. "A Jersey girl."

"I guess." She yawned again. "Satisfied?"

He kissed the top of her head. "For the moment."

She sat up in the bed, pulling the covers with her. "I think I better head home."

Dusty continued to lie where he was, watching her through narrow eyes. "Why don't you spend the night?"

"Can't. Got too much to do tomorrow."

"Am I being punished for asking too many questions?"

She glanced over her shoulder at him. "Don't be ridiculous."

"It just seems like everything was fine until I started asking questions."

She lay back down, folding her arms across his chest. "You're being paranoid. I just have a lot of work I need to get done. That's all, nothing more."

He watched her face for several long minutes before he said, "Okay." He moved from under her and got up from the bed. "Just let me get my clothes on."

He bent to pick up their clothes from the floor, and Mikayla watched him, knowing she'd ruined their perfect mood with her insecurities.

"What a rude host you turned out to be."

He stood and turned to her with a confused expression. "I beg your pardon?"

She stood on her knees and crawled across the bed to the edge and placed her arms around his neck. "Well, when you come to my place I offer you my shower before you leave."

He smiled. "Wanna take a shower?"

"Well, I was thinking, why don't we take one together. You know, to conserve energy."

His smile turned into the beautiful grin she loved

so much. "You know, I'm all about doing my part to conserve energy." He reached down and swooped her up in his arms and carried her into the bathroom.

When they pulled out of the horseshoe drive an hour later in Dusty's small sports car the loving mood was back.

Dusty told stories about growing up in the circus and what a shock the world was to him once he left it. Mikayla laughed all the way back to Miami and even when he arrived at her house she did not want the night to end.

"Wanna come in?"

He lifted an eyebrow. "I thought you had work to do."

"I do, but I'm home now. So I can play with my boy toy a little, and work a little, play a little, work a little."

"Boy toy?"

She laughed. "Oh, I'm sorry. My male amusement."

"How is that better?"

"It's not." She burst into a fit of laughter. "But I was hoping you would think so."

"I got your *boy toy*—right here!" He reached over and tickled her side and Mikayla fell into a fit of laughter.

Mikayla practically fell out of the car trying to get away. Leaning back in, she kissed him. "I had a great time today. Thanks for letting your family use your property."

"You were right, it makes sense. How can they get up on their feet if they can't make money?"

She smirked. "And you want them to get up on their feet, don't you?"

"Hell, yeah. I mean, don't get me wrong, it's been kinda fun seeing them all again after all these years, but it will be nice to see them leave as well so I can have my home to myself again."

"Selfish."

"Says the lady who lives in the city, far, far away."

Chapter 17

After Dusty dropped her off with a single kiss that promised more to come later Mikayla floated up the stairs to her front door. She paused and glanced back over her shoulder again, knowing he was long gone, but still feeling his presence.

She placed the key in the lock and opened the door. No one had ever made her feel the way Dusty did. When she was with him, the world was a different place. He made anything—no, everything, seem possible. He gave her hope.

It was a sensation even Mikayla didn't understand. It wasn't as if Dusty was the first man she'd thought herself in love with. In the old days, she'd fallen in and out of love all the time. But this was nothing like those mild crushes. This was an ever intense feeling of satisfaction. This was an almost euphoric happiness. This was real.

She closed the door and picked the mail up from the foyer floor, where it had fallen through the mail slot, and tossed it on the cherrywood console table. She leaned back against the door and closed her eyes, trying to remember the feel of Dusty's lips against her own.

He was only gone from her for five minutes and she was already missing him. She sighed to herself and moved away from the door. She had too much to do to continue acting like a love-struck schoolgirl, she silently scolded.

She started toward her office and then remembered to take the mail from the table into her office. She flopped down in her chair and began opening envelopes. She tossed the bills aside, took a quick minute to glance through the three magazines she'd received before tossing them in the trash and picked up the final piece of mail, which was handwritten with no return address.

With a small frown, Mikayla opened the envelope to find two pages inside. She unfolded the letters and one of them fell out onto the floor. She glanced down at the paper and froze in her tracks.

Mikayla felt a cold chill run through her entire body, from the top of her head to the tips of her toes.

It felt like a nightmare, although she knew she was still awake. She bent and picked up the paper, recognizing it as one of the show bills that was handed out to the patrons of the Godiva club.

Every week, the management put out advertisements featuring different girls, and this particular bill showed her as the featured dancer. The club had a strict rule about no cameras allowed inside, but this picture she'd posed for. And over the years had blocked it out of her mind.

Now, holding it in her hand, looking at it brought back all those memories. It was like she was standing on the stage of the Godiva club all over again. No, not all over again. It was more like she'd never left.

Taking a deep swallow, she remembered she was still holding the unread letter in her hand. She put the picture down and concentrated on the letter, hoping, praying it would offer some harmless explanation for the photo.

As she read the letter, she understood there was nothing harmless about it:

Hey, Tangie, it's been a long time. When you disappeared from the Godiva club it broke my heart, girl, thought I'd never get to see that pretty body of yours again. So imagine my surprise when I saw you at the Warren Ranch the other day. With Dusty Warren, no less! I wonder, does ol' Dusty know about your former occupation? Bet he doesn't. Bet you'd prefer he never found out. Because I like you, I am willing to make sure Dusty never finds out his author girlfriend is really a slut who will give it up to anyone.

Of course, it's your decision. You can either do what I say and Dusty is none the wiser, or ignore this letter and by the end of the week, not only Dusty but the entire city of Miami will know all about the secret past of the illustrious Mikayla Shroeder.

Think about it, and while you're doing that,

get $25,000 together within the next seventy-two hours. I'll be in touch with more information.
Signed,
An old friend

Mikayla reread the letter at least three times, feeling more and more shell-shocked with each reading. Her mind searched and searched the crowd she'd met at the ranch the other day, trying to find a familiar face. There were none. Of course, considering the number of men who came into the club on a regular basis, and that did not even include the occasional patron, there was no way she would ever remember every face.

But whoever he was, he recognized her. With all the changes to her life and appearance both inside and out, he still recognized her. As if the taint of her past bore some kind of invisible imprint only the lowlife's of the world could see.

Whoever he was, he was obviously with the circus. They were the only new people at the ranch. If it had been someone who worked for Dusty, that person would've come forward long ago, right?

She felt a migraine coming on. Going into her bedroom, she reached inside the drawer for some aspirin. By then her head was pounding, so she stretched out on the bed, feeling stress and exhaustion coursing through every inch of her body. Before long she'd fallen asleep.

The next morning, the sun shining on her face woke her and she realized she hadn't even closed the blinds the night before. She sat up on the bed, still fully dressed, and glanced at the clock on her nightstand, seeing that it was almost noon. Her whole body ached as if she'd tossed and turned all night, and she struggled to get her bearings. Suddenly, the memory of the letter and the show bill came rushing back to her.

Mikayla was no closer to an answer of what to do now than she had been when she'd fallen asleep. She stood and started across toward the bathroom when she spotted the tickets to the charity fundraiser she was supposed to go to with Dusty that night.

How was she supposed to face Dusty? It was too soon. She needed some time to think, time to sort things out in her head to find out what this person wanted from her. In truth, she didn't think that was any great mystery. He wanted money, of course. Wasn't that what all blackmailers wanted?

She reached for the phone on her desk to call Dusty's cell phone to cancel for the evening, but her hand paused over the receiver. He would want some explanation, but what could she tell him?

He'd dropped her off last night and everything had been fine. No, everything had been great.

How quickly life could change.

She had no idea what to say to him. The blackmailer was right in that regard. She would do pretty much anything to keep Dusty from finding out about her past.

Instead, she picked up the phone and called the one person who did know about her past and would never use it against her.

After a few rings, Kandi answered. "Hello?"

"Hi, it's me. Are you busy?"

"Just doing some shopping. Why?"

"I need to talk to you. Can you stop by here on your way home?"

"No problem. What's wrong?"

"I'll tell you when you get here. It's not something I want to discuss over the phone."

"Okay," Kandi said. Even through the phone line Mikayla could feel her curiosity. "I'll be right there."

Thirty minutes later, Mikayla watched Kandi pull into her drive. She pulled back the curtains and looked in both directions up and down the street, wondering if the blackmailer was out there.

She let the curtains fall and went to the front door to meet Kandi.

As soon as she opened the door, Kandi's worried eyes met hers. "What is it?"

As Kandi came in, Mikayla closed the door behind her and handed her the letter and the photo. Kandi's reaction came a lot faster than her own.

"Oh, my God!" Kandi looked between the letter and the show bill again and again. "Oh, my God! When did you get this?"

"When I got home a while ago, it was lying on the foyer floor with the rest of my mail. No return address, so whoever it is had to deliver it in person, which means he knows where I live."

Kandi's eyes widened even more. "I hadn't even thought about that! What if this guy is some kind of crazy stalker? You know you can't pay him, don't you?"

"Why not?" Mikayla asked, knowing full well she still had every intention of paying the blackmailer.

"If you do, he'll just keep coming back again and again. Don't you watch *Law and Order?*"

"But if I don't, he'll ruin everything I have worked so hard for."

The look that crossed Kandi's face caught Mikayla by surprise. "What's that look about?"

Kandi shook her head. "Nothing."

"Yes, something. What?"

Kandi sighed. "When we published your book, remember what I told you?"

Mikayla did remember and it did nothing to ease the aching feeling in the pit of her stomach. "Yes."

"You should've told everyone the first book was based on your life, then it would've all been out in the open and there would be nothing to blackmail you with. The way you did it set you up as some perfect target. People won't be as understanding now as they would've been then."

"Told you so? That's what you have to offer in the way of help. I called you over here because I'm terrified my world as I know it is about to end, and all you have to offer is 'I told you so'?"

Kandi moved close and wrapped her friend in a hug. "I'm sorry, you're right, you're right. This is not the time or the place for this. Okay, what do you want to do?"

Mikayla turned and walked back into the living room and sat down on one of the sofas. "I want to pretend like this never happened. I want to go back to feeling the way I did last night. But it's quite obvious I'm not going to get what I want."

"Then what are you going to do?"

"I'm going to pay whatever they ask."

"Didn't you just hear me? If you pay, they just keep coming back."

"I don't care! I can't let that stuff get out. Think about it. I'm a motivational speaker—in the Christian inspirational genre at that—who spends her days telling women they are more than just sex objects and then they all find out that is exactly what I used to be."

"Used to be." Kandi held up a finger. *"Used to be.* But you don't know that if you pay they will still keep their mouths shut."

"Like you said, they will come back wanting more later. To get more they will have to keep their secret a secret or else it'll lose its potency."

Kandi tilted her head and looked at her friend with a strange expression. "Do you hear yourself? You can't keep hiding from your own past, Mikayla. It's time to come forward with the truth before someone else does."

"But you just said the public would not be very sympathetic—"

"I said they would not be as sympathetic as they would've been back when you were first starting out, but it would still be better if you tell them and not some blackmailer trying to destroy you."

Mikayla stared down at the floor, trying to organize her thoughts. Kandi was right, of course, but Mikayla didn't know if she could survive the public scorn that would come with the announcement. And more importantly, the look in Dusty's eyes as he pushed her away from him. She knew beyond any doubt she was not strong enough to endure that pain. Dusty's rejection could be far worse than anything that had come before it.

"I'll think about it."

"You don't have long to think about it. He said tomorrow night."

"I know. I know."

Kandi crossed the room and sat down beside her on the sofa. "And…you know you're going to have to tell Dusty before then."

Mikayla shook her head. "No! I can't."

"Do you want him to learn about it on the six-o'clock news?"

"Why does it matter how he finds out—the outcome will be the same!"

"What do you mean?"

"You don't honestly think he will stay with me when he finds out, do you?"

"Actually, yeah, I do."

Mikayla made a disgusted grunting sound. "Then you're more delusional than I am."

Kandi simply stared at her friend for several long seconds before saying, "That remains to be seen. In the meantime, do you have any idea who it could be? He says he saw you at the ranch. Did you recognize anyone?"

"Don't you think I would've told you if I did?"

Kandi decided to ignore the harsh tone and continued. "And this…" She lifted the show bill. "How old is this thing? He must've been holding on to it for years."

Mikayla glanced at the picture. "Eight, to be exact. I posed for it when I was twenty."

"I feel so useless," Kandi moaned. "What can I do to help?"

Mikayla reached over and took her friend's hand. "You can do what you are doing right now. You can be my friend, you can listen and offer advice and..." She forced a smile. "You can help keep me from going insane."

Kandi smiled back. "I'll do my best."

In an effort to get her mind off things, Kandi talked Mikayla into ordering a pizza, and the two women ate and watched various clips of different shows. Five minutes of this and that, staying on a channel long enough to comment on the program before switching to something else.

It was almost six before Mikayla remembered her date with Dusty.

She sat up on the couch, from where she'd been resting her head against the armrest. "Oh, no! I'm supposed to go to a fundraiser with Dusty tonight." She glanced over to where Kandi was sprawled comfortably in the reclining overstuffed chair. "Will you call him for me and cancel?"

"Me? Why can't you do it?"

"I couldn't bare to hear his voice right now." She leaned forward and tried to look as sincere as possible. "Please, Kandi, just this once."

Kandi frowned at her, but still shook her head. "Just this once, but you can't keep hiding from him, Mikayla. You just can't. It's not fair to him or you." She pulled out her cell phone, talking all the while. "If you continue like this, the blackmailer wins and he's only just come on the scene."

Mikayla gave her Dusty's cell phone number and watched as Kandi dialed the number. "Hi, Dusty?"

"Yes, who is this?"

"This is Kandi, Mikayla's friend."

"Oh, hey, Kandi. How are you?"

"Fine, just fine. Um, Mikayla wanted me to call and let you know she will not be able to go to the fundraiser with you this evening."

"What's wrong?"

Kandi's eyes widened and she mouthed the question to Mikayla. Mikayla thought quickly and grabbed her stomach in mock pain.

"She's cramping," Kandi said into the phone.

Mikayla's eyes widened in humiliation. Shortly thereafter, Kandi felt a couch pillow hit her in the head.

"Sorry to hear that. Why didn't she call me herself?"

"Obviously you've never had cramps."

"Glad to say I have not," he answered drily.

"That's why you don't understand. When they are bad, they're *really* bad."

"Should she go to the hospital?"

"No, no. It's not *that* bad, just bad enough to stay in bed. In fact, I'm pretty sure she's asleep."

Mikayla, realizing the conversation was out of her control, could only shake her head.

"Think I should come over and stay with her?"

"No! Um, thanks anyway, but at this time, we women need other women. You understand, right?"

"Yeah, I understand. Okay, then, give her my love and let her know I'll call her in the morning."

"Will do." Kandi hung up the phone and fell back in her comfy chair. "Do not ever, ever, ever make me do that again."

"I won't. Thanks so much, Kandi. And just so you know, I was saying stomachache, not cramps."

"Same thing, right?"

Mikayla's eyes narrowed on Kandi's face, as she thought she heard a touch of sarcasm in the statement. But she was too relieved to be out of her commitment to Dusty to care. The pair went back to their channel surfing and it was well after midnight when Kandi climbed out of the reclining chair and headed home.

At the door, she turned to Mikayla. "Call me as soon as you hear anything, got it?"

"I will."

"And let me know if you want to go to the press and just make a statement about your past. I can set it all up for you, just let me know."

Mikayla nodded. "Don't worry, I will."

After watching Kandi pull out of the drive and head toward the freeway, Mikayla locked and bolted the door for the night. Then she crossed the room to the curtains, and hiding in the shadows looked up and down the street, searching for the blackmailer.

Whoever he was, he was keeping tabs on her. A part of her wanted to rush back out to the Warren ranch and take a look around to see if she could figure out who the blackmailer was. Not that she could do anything if she ever found him. But another part of her understood returning to the Warren ranch meant coming face-to-face with Dusty.

And Mikayla was honest with Kandi when she said

that she did not think she could do that. Not yet. Not until she had time to sort all this out and decide what to do next. Not until she had her past tucked away once more. Not until then could she continue with what up until that afternoon had been the perfect love affair.

As she drove down the freeway heading home, Kandi's mind was racing with possibilities. Things she knew she could do to help Mikayla, but her friend would never accept the help. For Mikayla, keeping up the persona she'd created for herself was more important than anything else. Even the love she had for Dusty.

And it was love. Kandi was certain. She'd known Mikayla for five years and had never seen the younger woman so enthralled by any man. Now she was about to throw it all away on some misplaced pride and some slimeball that had crawled out from under a rock and right into their lives.

She drove, battling her own conscience, but by the time she came to her exit her conscience had won. She found her cell phone in the bottom of her purse, and pushed the redial button.

"Hello?" Dusty answered again.

"Hi, Dusty. It's Kandi, Mikayla's friend again."

"Hey, what's up?"

"I need to talk to you."

"Okay. About what?"

"Are you busy right now?"

"Just doing some paperwork, why?"

"I'll come to your ranch. Give me about forty-five minutes."

"It's one o'clock in the morning."

"This is really important."

"Kandi, what is this about? Is something wrong with Mikayla? It's more than cramping, isn't it?"

"No, it's just I'd rather talk to you in person, if it's okay?"

"Okay, do you remember how to get here?"

"Yes, I'll see you in a little while. Oh, and Dusty, if you talk to Mikayla before I get there, please don't tell her about this."

"What is going on?"

"You'll understand once we talk. I'm just asking you to trust me for now. Can you do that?"

"I have no choice. Now I'm dying to know what you need to say so badly, you'll come out here in the middle of the night."

"Like I said, this is important. See you shortly."

The conversation ended, and even as she turned around and headed toward the Warren ranch, Kandi was still battling the part of her that knew Mikayla would consider what she was about to do a betrayal.

But she never turned the car toward home, and she never called to cancel the meeting with Dusty. She just continued on, hoping when this was all over and the blackmailer had been dealt with, Mikayla would see it in her heart to forgive her.

Chapter 18

It was the darkest hour of the night, and like a wolf stalking its prey, he moved through the circus camp in complete silence. Most of these people had been with his father since he was a young boy. Most of them were just good, honest, hardworking people who preferred an unusual lifestyle. In fact, he considered many of them family. But like every entourage there was always the occasional lost soul who would manage to attach himself to the group.

Those people were toxic not only to those around them, but to themselves, as well. They were self-destructive and came to the dangerous lifestyle hoping to end their own.

Unlike the patrons who sat in the bleachers and enjoyed the risky escapades with childlike glee, Dusty knew there were a thousand different ways the circus could kill. He'd met more than his fair share of those lost souls and remembered the ones his father had employed over the years, of which only a couple remained.

Dusty had a fair idea of who he was looking for, but he had to be certain. A few minutes later, he knocked on his father's trailer door and it swung open.

"Thought I heard someone out here," Kyle said with a cigar hanging off his lip.

Dusty knew he'd made almost no noise, which said a lot for his father's excellent hearing. Hearing that had been honed to perfection from years of living in harm's way.

"Surprised you're up this time of the night," Dusty said as he entered the trailer and glanced around. "And alone, as well."

Kyle shrugged. "Getting to be an old man, son. And Viagra can only do so much for a relationship. Most women feel I'm just not the great catch I use to be." He moved past Dusty and sat in a nearby wood chair. "But you didn't come all the way down here from the big house just to talk about my love life, did you?"

Dusty shook his head. "I need to ask you about a couple of people."

"Ask me what?"

"Well." Dusty pulled another nearby wood chair across from his father and sat down. "Louis—how is he?"

Kyle's eyes narrowed on his son's face. "Clean and sober for almost fifteen years now, if that's what you mean. Why are you asking?"

"You sure he hasn't maybe fallen off the wagon?"

"Considering I'm his ride back and forth to his AA

meetings, I can safely say Louis is off the sauce. What's this about, son?"

"Just wondering."

Kyle tilted his head to the side. "Don't tell me you're still sore about what he did to that old car of yours?"

Dusty hadn't forgotten about the incident the same way a person never forgot a broken heart. But like any other old ache it had been pushed to the back of his mind.

When he was seventeen, they were camping just outside a little town in northern Minnesota late summer. Dusty had been saving his money for years waiting for the right opportunity to buy his very first car, and he found it sitting in the front yard of a nearby farm. He used his savings to buy the beat-up Subaru for five hundred bucks. The car made horrible coughing noises, and by all accounts was butt ugly. But to Dusty it was a thing of beauty.

Until his father talked Dusty into letting Louis and Sam take it into town to pick up supplies. According to Sam, the ride into town had been trouble free, but while in town Louis had bought enough alcohol to replenish two liquor cabinets.

Sam thought little of it; everybody knew Louis liked his Scotch, and whiskey, and tequila and anything else he could get his hands on, but for the most part he drank on his time.

On the ride back, Sam fell asleep only to be awakened by Louis's scream as he ran them off the road and into a tree. When the whole story came out it was revealed Louis had gotten an early start on his drinking and by halfway through the road trip he was thoroughly drunk.

When Dusty heard about it, he'd been furious and attacked Louis. Kyle and three others had to pull him off the bigger man, and everyone had assumed his rage had been due to the fact his car was totaled in the crash. In truth, that part did hurt, but what hurt worse was Sam ended up paralyzed from the waist down and the incident was never reported to the police. Like Gypsies, carnies administered their own justice.

Louis was tossed out of the group for almost a year until he returned and announced he'd gotten clean and wanted to come home. Dusty had never gone along with the decision to take him back, but at the time, no one had cared about his opinion anyway.

"No," Dusty said with a slow head shake, "I'm not still sore about the car thing. Hey, how is Rick?" he asked, moving on to his next suspect.

Kyle shrugged. "Okay, I guess, why are you asking about these men?"

Dusty had caught his father's stiff movement, and wasn't about to just let it drop. "What do you mean, okay, you guess?'"

"I don't see much of him anymore."

That was noteworthy, Dusty thought. Kyle and Rick had once been bosom buddies, having started out in the carnival business together.

"Is he still training the horses?"

Kyle sat back in his wood chair and folded his arms across his chest. "I'm not answering another damn question until you tell me what this is all about."

Dusty considered how much to tell his father, and

then decided if he wanted his help he would have to tell him at least as much as he'd been told by Kandi.

"Someone here in this group is trying to blackmail Mikayla."

"What?" Kyle shot up out of his chair. "Who? Just tell me who and I'll kill him myself!"

Dusty stood, as well. "Calm down before you hurt yourself." He pushed his father's shoulders down until he was back in the chair.

"Blackmail her how?"

Dusty was not sure how Mikayla would feel knowing he'd shared such personal information, even with his father. "They found out something about her past, something she is not proud of, and now they are threatening to use it against her unless she gives him twenty-five thousand dollars.

Kyle's eyes narrowed. "Damn."

Dusty looked up. "What?"

Kyle sighed. "It's Rick."

"How do you know?"

"He's hard up for money and this is just his style." Kyle stood and turned away from Dusty. "I'm sorry, son. I didn't mean to bring you any trouble."

"If it is Rick, I can take care of this kind of trouble. I just need to be sure."

Kyle turned back to Dusty, and to Dusty's eyes it looked like his father had aged ten years in those few moments. "As you know, Rick has a gambling problem."

Dusty nodded. "Yeah, that's why he was top of my list."

"The last time we were in Miami he pissed off some

very powerful people with long memories. They want either their money with interest or blood. Almost from the moment we arrived and he got a look at the ranch and saw how well you were doing, he's been pushing me to ask you for money for him."

"Why didn't you say anything?"

"It never occurred to me he would go this far." He shook his head. "I should've seen it coming. I'm sorry, son."

"Stop apologizing," Dusty said, his mind already distracted by this new information. "You didn't do anything wrong. Where is he right now?"

"Should be in his trailer, but who knows."

"I'll find him." Dusty paused at the door and looked back at his father. He knew he should just leave it alone, but curiosity had gotten the better of him. "Hey, you never asked me what Rick found out about Mikayla."

Kyle looked into his son's eyes. "None of my business."

Dusty stood for several seconds, feeling like he should say something more, but not knowing what. Finally, he said, "Thanks."

Kyle frowned. "What are you thanking me for? Mikayla is a good woman, and you've worked so hard to get where you are, and by coming here I've managed to put all that in jeopardy."

Dusty had a thousand things to say in answer, but the conversation would have to wait for another day. Right now, he had to find Rick and deal with him before he got a chance to contact Mikayla again.

"We'll talk later," he said before leaving the trailer and closing the door behind him. He crossed the camp until he came to Rick's trailer and knocked on the door.

He started to call out his name, but feared if Rick knew it was him he would never open the door. He knocked again and still no answer.

Dusty was contemplating kicking in the door when he heard a car pulling in behind the trailer. He pressed his back against the trailer wall and waited.

After a couple of minutes, he saw the shadow of a stumbling man coming around the side of the trailer. He was fumbling with his keys and didn't see Dusty until he opened the trailer door and the lamplight spilled across his stoic form.

The expression on Rick's face was all the proof he needed. Dusty came up behind the man and pushed him into the trailer, slamming the door shut behind him.

Rick swung around with the intense fear of a trapped rabbit. Fear so obvious, the man was trembling.

"Sit your punk ass down." Dusty pushed him again so that he fell back on the couch.

Rick scrambled to sit up on the couch, and began to take in the situation. He forced a smile. "Dusty, man, what's going on? What's this about?"

"You know damn well what this is about!" He pulled up a folding chair and straddled it backward. He leaned forward. "Did you really think you would get away with it?"

"Get away with what?"

Dusty's eyes narrowed. "If you even try to deny it, I promise, when I get finished with you, your friends from Miami won't even recognize you."

Rick swallowed hard, his mind racing to find somewhere else to place the blame. Anyone would do well to keep Dusty off him. Surviving the night was his priority; he would worry about Leo's goons tomorrow.

"Dusty, I swear it wasn't my idea! I didn't even know the girl used to be a stripper! They told me to do that!"

"They who?"

"The men you were just talking about, they made me do it!"

Dusty just smiled. "Seriously?" He tilted his head to the side. "That's the lie you want to go with? *Really?*"

"It's no lie." Rick frowned, seeming confused by the smile.

Dusty shook his head. Then without warning he was standing and throwing the folding chair to the side. In two steps, he'd crossed the distance between them and had Rick by the collar of his shirt, lifting him from the couch.

"Dusty—no! Please, man, please! You don't want to do this! Please! I'm begging you, man!"

Dusty lifted his fist to send Rick into next week but paused when he realized the man was crying. Not a moaning, simpering whining kind of cry. But a full-on tears flowing like a river crying!

Dusty was so taken aback he dropped the man and Rick fell into a heap of weeping flesh at his feet.

Dusty shook his head at the spectacle. "You're about as pathetic as it gets, Rick." He turned and started to leave the trailer, but paused at the door. He turned to Rick, who was just beginning to realize he'd been left in one piece. "Understand something, Rick. I love this woman. I'm willing to do *anything* for this woman. Am I making myself clear to you?"

Rick nodded as if still confused by his sudden good fortune.

"If you so much as cough in her direction again, I will hurt you." He leaned toward the other man, and Rick sat back. "I—will—hurt—you."

Staring into the other man's eyes, Dusty was convinced he understood how close he'd come to danger. "Oh, and I want you off my property before daybreak or I'll have you arrested for trespassing."

As he walked out of the trailer camp and headed back up to his house, Dusty's mind was spinning. He glanced up at the star-filled sky. He'd always thought one of the best things about living out away from the city was being able to see so many of the stars at night. He'd thought about taking Mikayla out to one of the hidden spots only he knew about and making love to her under the stars, and then again as the sun came over the horizon.

There was so much he wanted to do with her, so many of his dreams he wanted to share with her. Places he wanted to see with her, things he wanted to experience with her.

But from what Kandi had told him, all that may be in jeopardy because she did not want to face her past. What Kandi had told him tonight explained so much. It was as if she'd brought him the final few missing pieces of a puzzle he'd been struggling to put together.

The mistrust of anyone, including him. The brief glimpses of pain he would see in her eyes when she thought he wasn't looking. The defensive wall she'd built around herself. Where it all came from, where it all started. He smiled to himself, thinking of the mangy mutt he'd come to love. Even Angel's presence in her life now made perfect sense.

From what Kandi had said, Mikayla would not thank her for sharing so much with him. But he was grateful to Kandi, more grateful than she would ever know.

Now that he had all the puzzle pieces he could concentrate on finding a way forward. Because contrary to whatever she believed, he was not about to let her just walk out of his life. Not now, not ever. He'd waited so long for her to show up, and now that she had he was sure that together they could conquer whatever obstacles stood in their way.

He was confident Rick would no longer pose a danger. The man might be stupid and greedy, but he wasn't suicidal. Of course, he could almost hear Mikayla's argument. What if there was another Rick somewhere, waiting to destroy all she'd worked for? He agreed with Kandi, it would be best if she spoke to the public and presented her story her way, rather than leave it to someone else whose motivation was to scandalize her name for money. But in the end, it would have to be her decision.

He dug in his pocket and toyed with his cell phone. He decided calling her was not the best idea. She would most likely ignore his calls.

As he reached his house, he walked in the back door, picked up his keys and headed right out the front. No, he decided, a phone call would not suffice. Mikayla had spent years building a fortress around her heart, and everyone knew there was only one way to bring down a fortress. You had to lay siege.

Chapter 19

Loud banging noises woke Mikayla. She sprang out of bed and began looking around for something she could use as a weapon.

After a few seconds her brain registered the banging was coming from the outside, not the inside of her house. Someone was banging on the front door. She glanced at the clock on her nightstand. Who would be banging on her door at five in the morning? Her eyes widened, wondering if the blackmailer had decided to go a different route to collect his reward.

"Mikayla! Open up!" Dusty banged on the door.

The sound of the familiar, husky voice lessened her confusion.

"Mikayla, I know you're in there! Let me in!"

She hurried to the front door and looked out the peephole to see a furious Dusty standing there. *What is he doing here?*

"Mikayla! I've been awake all night, I'm tired. Now let me in!"

"Go away!

"Open the door! Mikayla...I know about the letter and the pictures." There was no response for so long Dusty started to worry. "Mikayla?"

He heard movement from inside the house and waited, hoping she would open the door, but instead he heard a soft voice.

"You know?"

"Yes. Please, sweetheart, let me in."

"Kandi told you?"

"It doesn't matter. Do you hear me? None of it matters. Please open the door, I need to see you."

The door cracked open and her face appeared. "I never wanted you to know about my past."

"It doesn't matter." He tried to reach for her, but she pushed the door closed to a slit of space.

"It matters to me. I thought I'd left all that behind me. I thought that part of my life was over. And here it is all over again."

"I love you. And you love me. That's what matters— not some ancient history that doesn't have anything to do with who you are anymore."

"You don't understand."

"I understand more than you know, sweetheart. More than you know."

Mikayla leaned her forehead against the door and slid it shut. "Goodbye, Dusty. Don't come back," she said from the other side.

"Mikayla—I know who's responsible." The statement was met with silence. "Did you hear me? I know who is behind this blackmail and I promise you, baby, he's going to pay."

The door slid open a fraction. "Who?" The single whispered word almost broke his heart. Dusty could hear both the fear and bewilderment in the statement.

"His name is Rick Morgan. He's a horse trainer in my father's troupe." He tried to slide his hand between the door, but it was not open far enough. "In fact, we saw him the other day when we were visiting my dad."

"The guy you waved at?"

"Yeah, that's him. Sweetheart, open the door."

"Rick Morgan." She said the name as if expecting it to conjure a memory, maybe a disgruntled club patron, but as far as she knew Vega was the only one with a personal vendetta against her. Otherwise, there had just been too many men coming and going at Godiva, far too many to remember all their names and faces.

"Mikayla, you don't need to worry about Rick Morgan. He won't be bothering you again—I promise." He gently pressed his body against the door. "Let me in, Mikayla. I need to see you."

She peeked out the door once again, and he could see the tears in her eyes. He wanted desperately to take her into his arms, but she refused to allow him any closer.

"You were never supposed to know about any of this," she said, her voice cracking on the last word. "I tried so hard to rebuild my life. But you can't escape the past no matter how hard you try." The door slit shut again. "Goodbye, Dusty—and…thank you." Her muffled voice came through the door.

"Mikayla!" He banged on the door. "Don't do this! Mikayla! Open this damn door, now! I'm not leaving!"

He banged on the door again, but to no response. He banged again and again, and continued to bang until her next-door neighbor came out on the porch to see what was going on.

Knowing the nosy neighbor had probably already called the police, Dusty decided to leave. The last thing he wanted was to cause Mikayla any more trouble than she already had.

He moved down the stairs and back to his car. He sat in his car for several more minutes, hoping, praying she would come back to the door and let him in, but she never did.

As he drove back to his ranch, all he could think about was the hurt he'd seen on her face. He'd tried to make her understand he didn't give a damn about whatever came before him, but there was something he was missing. He could see it in her eyes.

Despite what he'd learned there was obviously much more he did not know. Some part of him wanted to try to beat more information out of Rick, but that would've been pointless. The man had told him all he knew; he'd been too frightened to lie.

So what now? How was he supposed to make the woman he loved let go of past hurts and look toward the future? How did you convince a person they didn't have to stay the person they were born?

If that were the case, he would've never left the carnival. He would've spent his life just as his father and grandfather had done.

An hour later he drove through the gateway of the ranch leading up to the main house, and the emptiness he felt in his chest became heavier with every turn of the wheels. He'd lived here for more than five years, but the past few months with Mikayla's presence had changed everything.

The place would never feel the same again.

He pulled to a stop in the horseshoe drive and saw his father leaning against one of the porch banisters with his hands deep in his blue jean pockets.

As Dusty turned off the car and climbed out, his father came down the stairs to meet him. "Well?" Kyle asked.

"She wouldn't even let me in."

Dusty was surprised by the hurt that crossed his father's face. "I'm sorry, son. She's a good woman."

Dusty raised an eyebrow at the finality of the statement. "This isn't over." He started toward the house. "I'll get her back, I just have to figure out how."

Kyle stood watching as Dusty climbed the stairs. "Son…"

Something about the tone caused Dusty to stop in his tracks. He turned to see his father watching him with a solemn expression.

"I've been thinking about what we were talking about earlier. And I just wanted to say, I'm sorry. I never meant to make your life hard. Hell, truth be told it never occurred to me that you were unhappy. I mean, I was just raising you the way I'd been raised."

"I know, Pop."

"Our people have been carnies for so long, I just never imagined you wanted anything different."

"I know."

"But I want you to know I am proud of you." He

gestured to the open fields around them. "Of what you've built here, of what you've made of your life."

Dusty could see the sincerity of his father's words reflected in his eyes and he swallowed hard. He wasn't sure how much more emotional turmoil his heart could take in one day.

"Thanks." The two men stood watching each other for a moment, and then not knowing what else to say Dusty turned and went into the house.

Porthos was lying under the foyer table and he barely lifted his head as Dusty entered. Dusty walked into the living room where Aramis was curled on the sofa. He gave only the smallest gesture of acknowledgment to Dusty's return. On the other side of the room, Athos had somehow wedged himself between a chair leg and the wall and his brown eyes watched Dusty, but he made no move to greet him.

Dusty realized he wasn't the only unhappy male in his home tonight. His dogs were missing their new queen, as much as he was missing his.

He went upstairs and slipped off his pants and shirt and climbed into bed. For the next few hours he lay in the dark, staring up at the ceiling. He had no idea how he could get Mikayla to talk to him, if he couldn't even get her to open the door to him.

She was hurting so bad, and he had no idea how to help her. He wanted to hold her, he wanted to put her head against his chest and just hold her. He wished he could somehow absorb her pain, take it into himself and relieve her.

Maybe it was good she had not let him in, because he didn't have the words to tell her what he was feeling.

But he had to find a way. He had to before it was too late.

He'd worked so hard to break the hard shell around her heart and he'd done it. He knew she cared for him as much as he cared for her. And, more importantly, she'd begun to trust him. Trust was an emotion that did not come easy to Mikayla. But she had begun to believe he would not hurt her. And with one stupid, careless, greedy act Rick had undone all that. She was now back to being the frightened woman he'd met six months ago. He could hurt Rick for that alone.

He sat up in the bed and turned on the lamp on his nightstand. He pulled out a slip of paper he'd tucked away just in case he needed it again and dialed the number.

He had a plan. It wasn't much of a plan, but it was all he had. It was his one shot, and if he didn't handle it right, it would be his last shot. Dusty knew time was not on his side. For every minute Mikayla was alone she replaced a brick in her wall of security. He had to do something now or else she would have the wall up between them again. And this time it would be indestructible. Mikayla was not the kind of woman to make the same mistake twice. Dusty knew it was now or never.

A woman answered the phone. "Hello?"

"Hi, Kandi, it's Dusty. This time I need *your* help."

Two days after receiving the blackmail letter, as the sun rose in the sky outside her window, Mikayla turned from where she'd been watching the sunrise and stretched. She glanced at the clock and saw it was almost seven in the morning. She hadn't slept all night. In fact, she hadn't slept in two nights. Not since Rick had hit her with his blackmail offer.

She kept replaying the night before in her head. The look of compassion in Dusty's eyes had been the answer to a prayer. It was just the look of understanding she'd hoped to find in his eyes if he ever found out. No judgment, just compassion. But nothing else about the situation was the same.

The cacophony of emotions racing through her brain was not expected. Her past was her past. She'd lived it—and thought she'd made peace with it. But when she'd opened that envelope and seen those photos it had been like a punch to the gut. She'd remembered taking them, of course. But still, looking at the woman in those photos had been like looking at someone else. Someone she didn't even know. And the shame she'd felt. She hadn't felt dirty when she posed for the pictures, so why now? After all these years?

It hadn't taken her long to understand what was generating such intense fear. It was the uncertainty of what Dusty would think.

The terror had taken hold of her heart and held it in a vise grip until the moment she opened the door and looked into Dusty's eyes. Then the feeling changed, but not to relief, which was what she should've felt. After all, Dusty said her past didn't matter, and she believed him. But the feeling was more like trying to balance on the edge of a cliff. Feeling as if any minute she would fall.

Even if she'd let Dusty in, she knew the feeling would not have gone away. It would always be. If she allowed her relationship with Dusty to continue she would spend her life waiting to fall. That would be unbearable.

It was better to let it end now. In a way, Rick had done her a favor. If he hadn't threatened her with those photos, she would've never experienced real fear.

When she'd faced down her knife-welding attacker in the dark alley all those years ago, she thought she'd known fear. But that was nothing more than the result of rushing adrenaline and anxiety. The thought of losing the respect of the man she loved, that was fear.

An hour later, she was just stepping out of the shower when her phone rang. She hurried into her bedroom to answer it. "Hello?"

"Oh, good." Kandi sighed. "You're awake. I need to see you, it's important."

"What's wrong?"

"Just meet me downtown at our coffee shop in half an hour."

"Okay, but what is this about?"

"I'll tell you when you get here."

Mikayla's mind was distracted from her own troubles as she tried to imagine what Kandi would need to discuss so urgently. She dressed in peach-colored safari shorts and a matching peasant top. She twisted her hair up and pinned it before slipping on some tan sandals.

She didn't even bother with any makeup or jewelry. She wasn't sure what was going on, but if Kandi needed her she didn't want to be late. She hurried out of her house, climbed into her sports car and pointed it toward downtown.

She pulled up in front of the coffee shop and was surprised by how empty it was. As she came closer and closer to the door, she had a feeling something wasn't right, and with every step the feeling grew stronger.

Inside, she saw Kandi sitting at a table alone. She opened the door and as soon as she did Kandi stood and came toward her.

"Hey, what do you need to talk—"

Before she could finish Kandi took her in a bear hug and whispered in her ear. "One day I hope you will forgive my recent betrayals, but I love you too much to let you spend your life regretting things you should've done differently."

Mikayla leaned back to look at her friend. "What are you talking about?"

Just then, the *what* appeared over Kandi's shoulder as Dusty stepped out from the short hall leading to the restrooms.

She shot Kandi a sharp glare.

Kandi whispered the word, "Sorry," and then hurried out the door.

Mikayla was frozen to the spot. There were a few other people in the shop. A young man was sipping a latté while working on his laptop. Another older man was reading a paper and drinking what appeared to be plain black coffee. And a couple close to the window was drinking coffee, while the toddler seated in the high chair between them sipped milk and toyed with a donut. The pair seemed in deep discussion and Mikayla knew no one would notice anything out of sorts if she turned and left.

Dusty stood where he was, waiting for her to decide. He looked so young and vibrant in his casual clothes, no one would guess he was a renowned veterinarian.

He wore loose-fitting jeans and a black T-shirt. The gold cross he wore sparkled against the black material. His short cropped hair had been recently cut, and from her point of view he looked good enough to eat.

It was so good to see him, she thought. She'd missed him like crazy over the past two days and had mistakenly thought she'd started the healing process. Apparently not. Because seeing him at that moment hurt as much as it had two days ago.

She knew she should turn around and leave, but the truth was she wanted to be with him, even if for a moment.

Once he realized she was not going to bolt, Dusty started moving in her direction. He stopped at the table where Kandi had been sitting and tossed a manila folder on the table.

Taking a deep breath she approached the table and the pair stood watching each other for several moments before Dusty said, "Don't blame Kandi, I asked her to do this."

"I'll take care of Kandi later."

"I needed to see you, and I didn't know how else to do it since you won't even take my calls."

"Well, I'm here now."

He gestured to the chair across from his as he sat down. He pushed the file across the table to her. "Here."

She frowned down at the folder, but did not take it. "What's that?"

He nodded toward the folder. "The brick wall standing between us."

She sat down and opened the file.

Chapter 20

In it were news clippings regarding her attack and the humiliating trial that followed and ended in a hung jury. Looking at the photographs of herself entering the courthouse, Mikayla felt as if she were looking at pictures of a stranger. So much had happened since then, so much had changed.

"Where did you find this?"

"A little research was all it took."

She looked up at him. "Why?"

"You needed to see it."

She closed the folder. "I don't need to see it. I lived it, remember?"

"Yes, and you keep telling yourself it doesn't matter when in fact, it matters a great deal."

Her eyes narrowed on his face. "Don't try to shrink me, Dusty. You're not qualified for the job."

"I beg to differ." He pulled the file back to himself

and opened it. "I think I know you better than you know yourself."

She arched an eyebrow and crossed her arms over her chest. "This should be interesting. Please, do go on."

"I think you blame Tangie for what happened to you."

"You're confused." She frowned. "I am Tangie."

"Yes, you are." He nodded.

She tilted her head to the side. "You speak as if she's someone else."

"Because in your mind she is."

"What are you talking about?"

"I'm talking about why you hide your past as if it's some kind of dirty little secret, when in fact it's the foundation of all you are. I saw you at that seminar, Mikayla. *Tangie* is the reason those women can relate to you. Whether you realize it or not, Tangie is the woman who takes the stage. Not Mikayla. Tangie. They know her—hell, they *are* her."

He leaned forward across the table. "Mikayla, you give so much of yourself, and yet, you hoard the best parts."

"Enough of this." She stood and turned to leave.

"See what I mean?"

His words stopped her in her tracks.

"Whenever we get too close to uncovering those old scars, you run and hide."

Reluctantly, she sat back down. "Why should I uncover my old scars, Dusty? I've spent years…*years* learning to live with my past, learning to accept my mistakes and move on. And now here you come, wanting to just dig it all up, like it's some kind of social experiment."

"But, sweetheart, that's just it. You haven't learned to live with your past. You've learned to hide it, you've buried it deep. And yes, you're right, I want to dig it up, expose it to the world and then you can release it forever."

She stared at the man she loved, feeling a sharp pain in her chest. What was he doing to her? All the conflicting emotions going through her head felt as if she would explode from the pressure. She didn't want to talk about this, she didn't was to rehash the past, and yet she knew she had to, or else the Ricks of the world would continue to have power over her. She had to if she hoped to have any kind of life with Dusty. And she did so want a life with Dusty.

She swallowed hard and pushed forward. "What are you trying to say, Dusty?"

"I think you should tell your story. I think you should identify yourself as the main character."

"What good would that do?"

"First of all, you wouldn't have to hide anymore."

Mikayla thought about that single statement. She'd been shielded for so long, she didn't even remember a time when she was not hiding some part of herself. She could only imagine the kind of relief it would bring, and the possible disdain and rejection.

"You're asking me to sabotage my career."

He shook his head. "I don't think it would. In fact, I think it would help."

"So I should risk undoing everything I've worked so hard for on the basis of an I don't think so."

He smiled. It was a small, sad smile. He looked at

her with compassionate eyes. "That's what trust is, sweetheart. Leaping without a net."

She huffed. "That's also called suicide."

"So what do you say?"

"If I say no, where does that leave us?"

"Wherever you want us to be. I'm here to stay, as long as you want me. I'm here." He reached across the table and took both her hands in his. "I love you, Mikayla, and that love is without condition. Know it."

"I do." She nodded, and the tears came without warning. Before she realized he'd moved Dusty came around the table and pulled her into his arms. The others in the restaurant gave the embracing couple a brief glance, before returning to their own pursuits.

Meanwhile, in a portion of the Warren ranch that went unused, a small makeshift tent had been set up in the underbrush. Rick sat inside, plotting his revenge. He couldn't leave Miami until things calmed down with Leo. He was already a day late for the new deadline, and he had no intention of being carried out of Leo's office in a plastic bag.

After Dusty left, Rick had gone to Kyle and pleaded for mercy, but Kyle had shown him none. Kyle informed him that after a lifetime of messing up with his son, he wasn't about to risk ruining their relationship forever for a gambling debt that wasn't even his. It seemed their lifelong friendship had met the end of the road.

Kyle's reaction brought home to him how serious things had spiraled out of control. That point was made clear when Rick left the ranch after his conversation with Kyle and noticed the car following him. He knew right away they were Leo's men and they had been following him all along. It took him almost two hours, but he was finally able to shake the tail and double back to the ranch. He knew even if Leo's guys searched the ranch it was so dense with forest they would likely never find him.

Rick thought about how to get enough money to not only pay off Leo, but set himself up for a long time. He knew between Dusty and Mikayla there had to be millions available. But he had nothing to offer that would guarantee payment.

If he went public with Mikayla's secret at this point, Dusty would know it was him. But at the same time, images of the unfortunate Mikey being carried out of the office by Leo's goons continued to run through his memory. He feared Dusty's wrath, but Rick felt dying at Leo's hands in such a brutal way was scarier.

Of the two, Rick had decided, Dusty would be the one he would have to take on. Not just for his refusal to help with his money problems, but Dusty had also cost him the one thing he valued in this world. His family. Or at least that was how he thought of the circus group.

When word had gotten around he was being put out, no one came to him to ask why. They seemed to all just accept if Kyle felt it was necessary to go to such extremes there must be a justifiable reason. So he was not even given the opportunity to explain his side of things. He'd just been cast out.

Of course, he could find another home with another circus, but where was he supposed to find a manager as indulgent as Kyle had been of his little bad habits?

No, Dusty had cost him more than just a financial

setback. He'd cost him his family. And for it all, Dusty would pay. If it meant taking down his beautiful Tangie as well, then so be it.

In downtown Miami Leo listened to the report from one of his men. He'd known Rick had no way of paying off the loan, but as he'd said, he liked the guy and wanted to give him a chance. Just in case, he'd put a tail on him and somehow Rick had managed to lose them, but not before he led him back to the Warren Ranch.

It had been an interesting discovery to realize Dr. Warren and Rick were connected. He never would've imagined the little weasel had those kinds of friends. But whatever the relationship it was not such he could ask for money from the rich veterinarian.

All morning his men had combed the typical hangouts for someone with Rick's particular affliction, and so far they had come up with nothing. It was as if the guy had just disappeared.

But now Leo knew he had to find Rick. Letting him get away again would set a bad precedent. It might give some the impression he was getting soft. And in his business all a man had was his reputation.

"Did you check out the ranch?"

"Tried, boss, but this guy came out of the animal hospital and started asking questions. I thought it would be better if we just left."

Leo nodded. He'd always taught his guys to avoid being noticed if possible and that included creating a scene that would cause people to remember your face.

"Well, he's got to be around here somewhere. Find him before he tries to leave the city."

"Will do, boss." The henchman turned to leave the room and paused. "Um, boss, when we find him...did you want us to bring him alive? I just ask because he'll probably put up a fight."

Leo's eyes narrowed. "I don't care if you have to bring him to me in pieces—just bring him to me."

The henchman nodded. "Right, boss." And then he was out the door, shutting it behind him. Leo sat in the empty office for several long minutes, thinking over different aspects of his life. He thought about all the men he'd killed or had killed over the years and the one time he decided to show a little compassion it came back and bit him in the ass.

"Well, one way or another," he said aloud, "Rick Morgan will have to die in the next few hours or my word will no longer mean anything."

Leo was a man whose entire livelihood was founded on his word. When Leo called you a *dead man*, you were.

Chapter 21

As she sat at her computer writing out the outline for her next seminar, Mikayla couldn't stop the smile that came to her face at the memory of Dusty.

The past few weeks seemed like idyllic paradise. Despite their conversation in the coffee shop, there had been no pressure from Dusty to go public with her story. They spent their days together either at his ranch or her house and spent their evenings wrapped in each other's arms.

Without the weight of her secrets holding her down, Mikayla felt like a new woman. It wasn't until she had nothing to hide that she realized her whole relationship with Dusty had been like living in a minefield. Afraid with every step the world would explode right in front of her.

And the knowing.

Dusty's knowing was like a deep breath of the freshest

air she'd ever breathed. He knew all the secrets of her troubled past and it had not changed even one aspect of their relationship. If anything, it had strengthened it.

Every once in a while he would ask her questions about her childhood or her life working at the Godiva club, but never even an ounce of condemnation in his tone. Just curiosity. He wanted to know her and her love for him grew deeper and deeper with each passing day. Never in a million years would she have imagined she could have a relationship like the one she shared with Dusty.

The dark cloud in her otherwise sunny world was the nagging feeling of standing on the edge of a cliff. It would not go away. No matter how she tried she could not shake the feeling something else was coming. Her new, wonderful life was allotted a certain amount of time to exist, and the clock was running out.

The night Dusty showed up at her house demanding entrance, Mikayla had thought back over the man she'd seen briefly at the circus and realized some part of her must've recognized Rick Morgan then. Out of all the people that had been around, he'd been the one who caught her attention.

After Dusty told her who the blackmailer was, the final piece of her mental puzzle fell into place and she could see the horse trainer sitting at the bar of the club, watching her with those hungry eyes. He'd looked at her the same way the last time she saw him.

She couldn't help wondering how she'd been so lucky to not have met any former club regulars up to this point. Of course, she had always been careful to put out very little information about herself, but in the

Internet age anyone could find out anything. Dusty and Kandi were right about that much. Until her whole story was revealed to the world, she would never be safe. But what they did not understand was that what they thought of as simply the details of her past were, for her, scars as real as if they showed on her flesh.

Announcing her attack to the world would open those wounds and all the ugly puss of that night would ooze back into her life. She loved Kandi and Dusty both, but neither of them understood what they were asking. They wanted her to *deal* with it.

They really thought it was simple. She would just deal with it and move on. When in fact what she would be doing was opening Pandora's box, and once it was open she wasn't certain she could close it again.

Not to mention what the press would do with the story. Before all was said and done she knew she would be painted as a whore. Not only a whore, a whore who had the audacity to try to preach to others about their pasts and their mistakes.

And her fans, what would they think? Dusty seemed to believe they already sensed her struggles, if not the specific details; and they held the strong belief that she had endured and survived something. Dusty believed they would forgive her because they could relate to her.

Mikayla was not so sure. She knew some of her fans looked up to her with an almost heroinelike adoration, and no one wanted to see their heroine humanized. She was supposed to be above reproach, springing from the earth as a fully developed, emotionally stable guide.

Now she sat working out the details for her next

seminar and everything that had happened over the past few weeks seemed to be working its way into her thoughts. When she sat down to write it, the guideline had been entitled *Finding the Fighter in You*. And as she wrote it, the plan had changed so she was considering renaming it *Finding the Lover in You*. That's what Dusty had done. He'd helped her find the lover in herself.

The phone rang and she picked it up. "Hello?"

"Hey, what are you doing?"

She smiled. "Working. What are you doing?"

"Feeling pretty good about myself. Have you got a couple of hours to come down here? I want to show you something."

She glanced at the clock. It was almost noon. "Okay, want me to pick up some lunch on the way?"

"Sounds great. See you in a little while."

As she hung up the phone, Mikayla wondered what could not wait. Almost an hour later, after stopping at her favorite sub shop for a couple of twelve-footers, Mikayla drove through the gates of the Warren ranch, rounded a corner and took the paved path leading to his house.

Hearing the car approach, Dusty came out on the porch to greet her. He was dressed in his typical blue jeans and plaid shirt and he stopped and braced his weight against the porch rail, waiting for her to turn the car off.

As she stepped out of the car, he smiled and came down the stairs. Without warning, he scooped her up in his arms and hugged her close. "Missed you."

She laughed. "I just saw you yesterday."

"I know, almost a whole twenty-four hours." He

kissed her lips, a soft kiss turned passionate. She surrendered her mouth to him, giving him the access he always desired.

He set her on her feet, but he never let go of her as his busy hands began to roam over her body, cupping her round bottom.

She stepped back out of his reach, but the dreamy expression on his face told her it did little to curb his lust.

She held up the bag containing the sandwiches. "Hungry?"

His eyes roamed over her body. "You have no idea."

She shook her head. "Uh-huh. You did not take me away from my work to drive all the way down here just so you can get some."

He smiled. "You'll get some, too, I promise."

Her mouth twisted in a smirk. "You're joking, right?"

He shook his head. "No. But you're right, that is not the reason I wanted you to come down here." He took the sandwich bag from her, turned and headed into the house. "Follow me."

Dusty opened the door and let her go ahead of him, and then he led the way through the house, dropping the sandwich bag on the counter and heading out into the backyard. Athos, Porthos, Aramis and Angel played, chasing balls being thrown out by Sam.

Sam gave a brief welcoming wave to the couple before returning his attention to the dogs clambering for the ball he was holding.

"Angel!" Mikayla called to her dog.

Angel heard the call, but continued to follow the ball with the other dogs. Mikayla was crushed by her indifference.

"She barely noticed me."

Dusty put his arm around her shoulders, sensing her sadness. "Believe it or not, it's a good thing."

"It doesn't feel like a good thing."

"I know, but it's for her own good and yours, as well."

She looked up at Dusty with hurt eyes. "I brought her to you to be taught obedience, not to turn her against me."

He laughed. "No one has turned her against you. She's just discovered she likes being a dog, and being with other dogs." He kissed her forehead. "Trust me, when you take her home she will give you all the attention she has to offer. But for right now she's just being a dog—which is good." He took her hand and tugged until she sat down beside him on the stair.

Once they were seated, Dusty took both her hands in his. "For too long, Mikayla, Angel's been in guardian mode. She needs to be allowed to be just a dog. Can you understand?"

She frowned. "You're like a broken record. You said this before."

"It's the truth and the reason she couldn't be trained before now. Because no matter what the setting was, if you were there she automatically assigned herself the alpha dog, your guardian and protector. And there is only ever one alpha."

Mikayla glanced over her shoulder to where her dog was playing, and began to see her for the first time.

She was always playful, but Dusty was right, she had a sort of bully thing going on that Mikayla had never understood.

"Mikayla, if you ever hope to have anything like a normal home with her, you are going to have to establish yourself as the alpha of your pack."

"What pack? It's just the two of us."

He made a gesture to dismiss the statement. "Anything more than one is a pack."

He nodded toward the group of dogs, now fighting over the ball. At the moment, Porthos had it and was running away, little Aramis yapped up a storm, cutting through his legs and tripping him, which allowed Angel to attempt to steal the ball. Athos came out of nowhere and started tugging on it, as well. The two dogs were making such a loud, growling noise Mikayla became concerned.

"Is that okay? It sounds like they are fighting."

He watched the dogs. "They're fine. It's all in good fun."

Mikayla and Dusty sat watching the dogs get a workout as Sam put them through run after run, and it was obvious the dogs were loving every bit of it.

After a while, Mikayla said, "I thought you said you prefer to train Angel alone."

"That was before I saw her with these dogs. With the dogs at the kennel, she'd assumed the role of alpha, but that entailed leading a revolt and escaping under the fence every day. For some reason, with my dogs it's different. Even though she thinks she's the alpha, they work together like a team." He gestured to the dogs. "As you can see."

He glanced at her. "I wanted you to see she is as you said, very smart, and extremely stubborn, but she is trainable."

Mikayla, still reeling from Angel's lack of interest, wanted to take her dog home. "It's been almost eight weeks. Can I take her home soon?"

He nodded. "Just give me a couple more days with her."

Sam put the toys up and the dogs followed him to the toy bin before they realized their afternoon exercise was over. Sam came over to the stairs and rested against the railing.

"Hey, Mikayla. How are you?"

"Fine. You're doing a great job with Angel, Sam. I just want to thank you."

Sam smiled. "No thanks needed, just doing my job." He looked at Dusty. "If you don't need anything else, I'm going to head back down to the kennel."

"All right, see you later." Dusty stood and offered his head to Mikayla. "Wanna eat?"

"Yeah, I haven't eaten all day and I'm hungry as a bear."

As he led the way back into the kitchen, Dusty asked. "Why haven't you eaten all day?"

She shrugged. "When I get caught up in a project time flies."

"What project?"

"I'm working on a new seminar."

He grabbed two cans of soda from the refrigerator and together they sat down at the table. "Really? What's it about?" Dusty asked, tearing open his sandwich.

She looked at him. "No offense, but I don't like to discuss my work while it's in progress."

He frowned, slightly hurt. "And after I just shared my work in progress with you?"

She bit her lip. "Sorry."

"No biggie," he said, biting into his sandwich. After a while, the noises coming from the backyard got quiet and Dusty realized the dogs had taken off to explore some other part of their domain. "It just means it will be more interesting when I see you give the presentation."

Mikayla ate her sandwich, practically cooing with pleasure. "I swear this shop makes the best sandwiches in the world!"

"It is good," Dusty agreed, taking another bite of his own.

Once she was halfway finished, Mikayla mostly just picked at the sandwich as other thoughts ran through her mind. "Dusty?"

"Hmm?" Dusty answered on the last little bit of his sandwich and pushed the plate aside.

"You never said anything more about Rick."

"What do you mean?"

"Well…you never said what happened when you confronted him."

Dusty looked at her. "I told you, Rick won't be a problem anymore."

Her eyes widened. "Okay, *waaayyy* too cryptic. What do you mean, he won't be a *problem anymore?*"

"Just that." He opened his soda and took a drink. "I made sure he understood if he tried his little stunt again, it would be the last thing he did."

She watched him for a few seconds. "He believed you?"

"Yes."

"Why?"

Dusty looked into her eyes. "He has reason to."

For the first time since she'd met Dusty, Mikayla looked into his eyes and saw nothing resembling compassion. There was a hardness, a coldness she had not known existed.

"Oh," was all she could manage. She wanted to forget that look. The man she'd just glimpsed was not the Dusty she loved.

She glanced toward the back door. "Where is he now?"

Dusty shrugged. "I don't know."

She turned back to Dusty. "You kicked him out—didn't you?"

He frowned at her. "Of course. What was I supposed to do? He was trying to blackmail you, remember?"

"But the circus is his home, Dusty."

He tilted his head to the side as if studying some strange creature. "The man was threatening to destroy your whole life and you feel bad because he lost his *temporary* home?"

She toyed with her sandwich some more. "You're right. You're right. Why should I care?"

"Exactly."

A tense silence settled over the pair, until Dusty spoke. "Look, you don't know Rick like I do. He was bad news. In case you were wondering, the reason he was blackmailing you was to get money to pay off his gambling debts. He owed a lot of money to some real bad dudes. I told him to get off my property not just because of what he was trying to do to you, but for my father, as well. Imagine if those people showed up here looking to collect their money?"

"I understand."

"I hope so. Because Rick Morgan is a damn fool, and if it wasn't these guys it would be someone else. Eventually his luck is going to run out and I don't want anyone I love anywhere near him when it happens."

Chapter 22

As the evening wore on and the conversation moved away from topics of contention such as Angel's training and Rick Morgan, the couple settled back into their comfort groove and ended the night with the season finale of *Dancing with the Stars*.

Dusty convinced Mikayla to stay the night. Not that it took much convincing—just a couple of properly placed kisses and the promise of more to come.

Later, as she lay curled in Dusty's arms, listening to his steady breathing, Mikayla's mind was still racing with her conflicting emotions and thoughts. For some reason, Dusty's recent success with Angel did not bring her the satisfaction she had hoped for, and for the life of her she could not understand why not.

For years she'd searched for someone, anyone who could bring Angel into line. Giving her up had never been an option, so her only hope had been someone capable of training her. And now Dusty had found a way to connect with her pet, but instead of making her happy, she was feeling…the emotion she decided could only be described as fear.

"What are you thinking about?" Dusty's seductive voice came out of the dark.

"I thought you were sleep," she whispered.

"How can I sleep when your whole body is radiating with tension? What's wrong?" He pulled her closer against her side.

She sighed. "Not sure." She turned on her side, folding her arms on his chest, and looked for his face in the dark. Soon her eyes adjusted and she found him watching her with those compassionate eyes she found such peace in.

"I don't know how to explain it, but…watching Angel today with the other dogs… I don't know, it's just…"

"You're bothered she didn't come to you right away?"

"I guess." She frowned. "Is that silly? To be jealous about a dog?"

"No, not when a dog means as much to you as Angel does."

She smiled remembering. "She rescued me, you know."

"Yes, I know. Kandi told me."

"And then even after the EMS took me away, she followed and stayed with me from the hospital to the hospice, just like a guardian, always there, always protecting, even at the risk of her own safety. That's why I named her Angel. She's my guardian Angel."

He laughed. "I admit when I first met you and got a

look at her, I couldn't see anything *angelic* about her. But I understand how you feel."

"I never understood why she was so determined to stay with me. I still don't."

"Dogs sense things about us, things we humans can't see on the surface. They survive by instinct, so their instincts are much more connected to nature. She knew you needed her, and she needed you."

"I did need her. When I woke up in the hospice, I was so weak. I could hear the nurses discussing my impending death, as if I were already dead. And I didn't care. I think I would've died, if I hadn't heard them talking about her and how she was hanging around. I was so scared she would end up in the pound and be put down all because she did not want to leave me. She gave me a reason to get well. So I could take care of her."

There was a long silence, and then Dusty spoke. "Marry me, Mikayla."

"What?" She sat up, not believing what she was hearing.

"I love you more than I ever loved anyone, and with every moment I just love you more. Marry me. Be my wife."

"Where did this come from?"

Even in the dark, she could see his confused shrug. "Hell if I know, I just know I want you forever. Marry me."

She patted his chest. "Tell you what. Close your eyes, and go to sleep and we'll talk about this in the morning."

"I'm as awake as you are. I know what I'm saying. Marry me." He sat up in the bed. Mikayla watched the covers fall to his waist and her mind shifted to other thoughts.

He arched an eyebrow. "We'll get to that later," he said as if reading her thoughts. "Right now, I need an answer. I'm serious. I love you and I know you love me. So, say yes."

"It's not that simple."

"Why not? What's standing in our way? I know your secrets, and you know mine. I know your faults and you know mine."

She frowned. "What faults?"

He smiled. "Sweetheart, as much as I love you, you're not perfect. Take this Angel thing for instance. I bet you still haven't realized why it's bothering you that I was successful in training her."

She looked down so he would not see the truth in her eyes, but it didn't matter. He continued as if she had spoken the words. "Okay, I'll tell you. For the past five years, Angel has been your ally, your confidante, your protector. In fact, she's been the *perfect* secret keeper."

He huffed. "Her bad behavior was your assurance she would always be there to keep your secrets. After all, no one else wanted to deal with her. She rejected anyone and everyone who tried to get close to you, allowing you to keep your little bubble securely in place." He leaned toward her and smiled. It was such a beautiful, seductive smile, Mikayla found her mind floating back to other things. But his next words broke the spell.

"But I'm getting close."

She looked up at his eyes and saw some certain knowledge. An almost smug assurance.

"You can feel it, can't you, baby?" He reached forward and pulled her to him. "For the first time, someone has managed to get past the security perimeter, past the guard dog, and you feel it. I'm coming for your heart, Mikayla, you know it, and it scares the mess out of you."

He lay back, pulling her over his chest. "So, you might as well marry me. Because I'm not going to give up."

"But you already have my heart," she whispered.

He shook his head. "No, that's a decoy. A small portion of you that you give to everyone. I want that part of you no one gets to see. I'm greedy." He kissed her neck. "I want Mikayla *and* Tangie."

She pushed up off his chest as a spark of anger shot through her. Just as quickly he slid her hands to her sides, bringing her back down on top of him. "You heard me. I want the whole woman. I want your passion, Mikayla. I want your pain, your pleasure, I want to share it all."

She pushed to get up, but he countered her every move. "I told you there is no Tangie anymore—let me go, you son-of-a-bitch!" she snapped.

His eyes widened. "Are you sure? Because I've never heard ultrapolite Mikayla use that kind of language."

Her eyes narrowed and she stopped struggling. "Let. Me. Go," she bit out.

He shook his head, watching her with solemn eyes.

"Never." With one quick motion, he flipped and they had switched positions. "I want all of you. Marry me."

"No!"

He smiled at the pouty expression on her face. He

leaned forward and placed gentle kisses along her jaw line. "Say yes."

"No."

His smile widened as he realized the "no" was less emphatic. He pushed his growing erection against her soft inner thigh. "Marry me, beautiful. I promise you'll never regret it."

This time all she could do was shake her head in response, even as her thighs parted, giving him access to what they both desired. Dusty continued to place gentle kisses along her neck, behind her ear, savoring every ounce of her delicate skin.

She moaned and tugged at her arms. He released his hold on her so she could wrap them around him. With the freedom of motion given, Mikayla wrapped her whole body around him, pushing herself up against him, trying to pull him inside her.

It took every ounce of his strength, but Dusty held himself away from her. "Say yes."

Mikayla wrapped her legs around his hips and the action opened her body to him. Dusty could feel the heat of her center tempting him, calling for him, but still he held himself away.

"Say yes, baby. That's all you have to do. Say yes."

Mikayla looked up into his eyes, her own filled with love and lust, and Dusty knew no matter what was said this night, he would never let this woman go, not in this lifetime.

"Yes," she whispered, "now, make love to me."

That was all the encouragement Dusty needed. He pushed against her center, feeling her hot wetness pull him in. He stopped and, reaching into the nightstand, donned a condom.

Dusty covered her body once more, pulling her legs over his hips, and drove himself deep inside her body. The tight opening sucked him inside and he could feel her body convulsing even before he'd reached his destination.

She shook and shivered as the climax took hold of her. Dusty was helpless to fight it as he was swept up in the current and his body jerked once, twice then his seed was spilling inside her.

He collapsed on top of her, his heart pounding against his chest. Her sweet smell filled his nostrils with renewed need. This was as close to paradise as any man could find on earth, he decided.

Dusty wrapped her in his arms and when he found the strength, he rolled onto his side. "I hope you know I'm holding you to that yes."

She smiled against his chest, then as if to torment him, her warm tongue dashed across his nipple. "I know."

Dusty kissed the top of her head and moments later he fell asleep, imagining what a life with Mikayla would be like. Never dull, he thought, and soon he was sound asleep.

Mikayla lay awake for some time after. She was going to marry Dusty. Her mind needed time to accept she had found him. The man she was meant to be with. She'd never imagined he even existed, and now she lay with him.

If she were honest, Mikayla knew Dusty was right. The unexplained fear she'd been feeling almost from the moment she met him was the knowledge this man could get past her barriers, and he had. More important, he'd seen beneath the surface, the darkness, the pain, and he still wanted her. Up until now the only people she'd had to share her soul with were her agent and her dog. But Kandi was right, it was not enough.

She needed a partner, she needed a lover, a friend, and Dusty was all of those things. She hoped she could be whatever he needed, as well.

The next morning the pair glided around Dusty's kitchen in a silent state of perpetual happiness. Neither spoke of the night before, but they both thought about it and shared knowing looks.

As Dusty was buttering an English muffin, he heard a muffled thump against the front door. "The paper—I'll be right back."

Mikayla, who was carefully scrambling the eggs so not to burn them, nodded as he left the kitchen.

A few minutes later Dusty walked back into the kitchen, but the smile on his face was gone, and his caramel skin had faded as if some of the blood had been drained from his face.

Mikayla turned the stove off. "What is it?" She walked over to him and then he looked at her and the sorrow in his eyes warned her she did not want to know whatever he'd just found out.

"I'm sorry, sweetheart. I didn't believe he would do it."

She frowned, but took the paper from his hands. Below the fold was a special-interest story about her. She took the paper and sat down. Dusty came to stand beside her and instead of reading the paper, he watched her expression.

After a while she shook her head. "No, it wasn't Rick. See?" She held up the paper and Dusty forced himself to look at the paper.

It didn't take long to realize the article was written by a reporter who'd been onto the story for some time. Long before the blackmail note.

"I guess you were right." She took Dusty's hand, which was resting on her shoulder, and rubbed it against her cheek. "The truth can't stay buried forever."

Meanwhile, in downtown Miami, Rick was sitting in the bus station reading the same article. He balled the paper in his hands, trying to hide his rage. Some jackass reporter had stolen his insurance policy right out from under him. His ace had been played and now he had nothing to bargain with. He'd hid out on the ranch as long as he could once the deadline had passed, hoping Leo's henchmen would stop looking for him long enough for him to escape.

He glanced at the clock on the wall. His bus would be leaving in thirty minutes, but every minute he was in town was one too many. He tossed the paper on the seat next to him and noticed a nice pair of shoes come into his line of vision.

He swallowed as his eyes went up and he found himself staring into the face of one of Leo's goons. Soon another came to stand beside him and Rick felt his whole body shaking.

"Hey, Rick," The first goon, smiled at him. "Leo's been looking for you."

Chapter 23

Later that week, Dusty and Mikayla stood together, waving goodbye as the circus caravan of trailers and trucks rolled through the gates of the Warren ranch.

Kyle drove up alongside them in his beat-up Impala. "Late August of next year, right?"

Dusty was tempted to ask his father to stay, but he knew the old man would never be happy sitting in one place for too long. Instead, Dusty nodded, pulling Mikayla closer against his side. "That's the time frame. We'll send an invitation when we have the details worked out."

Kyle smiled at Mikayla. "It has been an absolute pleasure to meet you, my dear."

She returned the smile and said, "You, as well." She walked over to the car and placed a kiss on his forehead. "Thank you for allowing me to see my first circus."

Kyle laughed. "The first of many, I hope. Who knows,

maybe one day you can travel with us for a while—
maybe write a book on us."

"Sounds like a great idea."

Dusty took her hand and pulled her back against his
side. "Um, I don't think so."

Kyle shrugged. "Just a suggestion. Think about it."
He winked at Mikayla and rolled on through the gate.

Mikayla looked at Dusty. "You're probably happy to
see them go so everything can return to normal."

Dusty frowned. "Not as happy as I would've thought.
Having them here reminded me of all the good times
we had. Somehow I'd forgotten all that and just focused
on the bad parts of it."

Her smile faded. "I know what you mean."

Dusty looked into her eyes, and he knew she did.

He glanced back and saw the hospital staff standing
outside, watching the group as they disappeared down
the narrow dirt road leading away from the ranch. He
clapped his hands. "Back to work, everyone."

Taking Mikayla by the hand, he started walking back
toward his house. Mikayla looked up at the large house,
thinking about the first time she'd seen it.

"Think you can get used to living here?" Dusty
asked, following the direction of her eyes.

"I think so." She smiled at him.

The pair walked on in silence a little longer before
Dusty said, "Thank you."

She looked up at him with a confused expression.
"For what?"

"For helping me to accept my family." He lifted their
entwined fingers and kissed the back of her hand.

"You did that all by yourself."

They walked in silence a little longer. "Are you going to be all right?"

"What do you mean?"

"Now that the truth is out."

She looked off into the distance, where four dogs were racing toward the stables, and smiled.

Dusty followed her eyes, but there was no smile to be found on his lips. "Aww, hell." He pulled out his cell phone and punched in a contact. "Hey, Sam, the *fantastic four* are heading to the stables to harass the horses. Can you—thanks, man." He hung up the phone.

He tucked the phone back into his pocket, having never let go of Mikayla's hand. "Have I told you what a bad influence she is on my dogs?"

She laughed. "No, but you really didn't have to. It's kinda obvious." She leaned over and kissed him. "And since we're handing out thank-yous, I have one for you."

"Really? And what would that be for?"

"That." She nodded in the direction of the stable. "In many ways, Angel and I are alike, you know. I think maybe that is why we ended up together."

He frowned. "I take offense at you comparing my beautiful fiancée to that mangy mutt."

"Seriously. The night we met in that alley was a turning point in both our lives. A chance to give up a hurtful past and start over. I thought once the scars healed I would be fine, but there were deeper wounds I'd never dealt with." She stopped and turned to face him. "You helped me to face the demons of my past and exorcise them once and for all."

He placed a gentle kiss on her forehead. "It was no

less than what you did for me." As they continued to walk, he slowly turned their bodies, heading in a new direction.

She looked up at him. "Where are we going?"

"It's a little pond over here I've been dying to show you. The water temperature is almost always perfect for swimming."

She pointed over her shoulder toward the house. "But I don't have a bathing suit."

His pace picked up to a light run and, looking back over his shoulder at her, he winked. "Trust me. You won't need one."

REQUEST YOUR FREE BOOKS!

2 FREE NOVELS PLUS 2 FREE GIFTS!

KIMANI ROMANCE

Love's ultimate destination!